The Baby and The Rock Star

ROCK STAR KISSES, BOOK TWO

Veronica Blade

Crush
PUBLISHING

Gardnerville, Nevada

The Baby and The Rock Star

Crush Publishing, Inc
Gardnerville, NV 89460
www.CrushPublishing.com

Crush Publishing, Inc name and logo are trademarks of Crush Publishing, Inc and are used only with its permission.

The places, characters and events portrayed in this book are fictitious. Any similarity to real persons, living or dead, is coincidental and not intended by author.

ISBN 978-0-9995994-6-4

Cover design and layout by Rose Nomura

Printed in the United States of America

The Baby and The Rock Star
ROCK STAR KISSES, BOOK TWO

EXCERPT

His smile widened and he used his thumb to brush a stray hair off my cheek. "You're ridiculous, you know that? It's kind of cute how you pretend you're not mysteriously drawn to me."

I licked my lips. He was right. It didn't necessarily follow that he needed to know how right he was. For one thing, that would be humiliating. Second, if he returned even half the lust for me, we were in big, big trouble. I could still speak the truth without confirming his assumption. "Sebastian, I swear on my mother's grave that I absolutely do not like you."

He pressed his lips together and brought his other leg forward, bringing his body flush against mine. "I don't like you either. So what are we going to do about it?"

I flattened my palms against his stomach, but my brain somehow misfired and instead of pushing him away, my fingers splayed over his muscles. The pressure of his fingertips at my hips compelled me closer and I held my breath. No way would he kiss me. I mean, I was crabby, pregnant and hormonal. Plus, he'd outright admitted to not liking me. Not that I could blame him. Right now, any woman in a ten-mile radius had to be more attractive than me. So what was he up to?

I lifted my chin to meet his smoldering gaze, but my eyes drifted to his lips. He inched closer and I squirmed until I was up against the counter facing him. His hands skipped upward to press against my waist, then spread out as if they couldn't bear not to cover every inch of me. I hadn't been touched like that by a man since... well, since my drunken hook-up with Sebastian two months before. I melted against him, hooking the finger of one hand through his belt loop and the other sliding up his chest to wrap around his neck.

Keeping his gaze trained on me, he levered his hips against mine so slowly I could feel everything from his hip to the zipper on his pants. My mouth parted and his mouth crashed down on mine. I devoured the kiss with a hunger that consumed me. This was nothing like the kisses I'd had with him before. This was loneliness and need, betrayal and fear, all rolled up with a healthy dose of lust and hate. I stretched up on my tiptoes and my arms overlapped around his neck, squeezing him closer. Our tongues tangled and the craving for more burned through my soul.

He pulled back just enough to whisper against my lips. "I was right. You're like liquid fire."

For my husband

who is my biggest cheerleader
and always there for me

♥

CHAPTER ONE
★ Sebastian ★

Violet was sitting so close to me, I could count her freckles.

As pretty as she was, I didn't want her in my house. We should've arranged a different meeting place so I could leave anytime. Fat chance of getting rid of her before she finished going through her dreadful list. At least I'd had the sense to offer her a kitchen chair, as opposed to the stuffed chairs in the living room where she'd probably be more comfortable, and likely stay longer.

She sure smelled good though. When I scooted my chair toward the other end of my dining room table, her sweet scent became fainter and I could concentrate again.

"I'm confident we can turn this around. A few weeks from now, you'll look like such a saint, mothers everywhere will be practically throwing their daughters at you." She squinted at her notebook filled with bullet points. Her To-Do list should have been retitled Fifty Ways to Torture Your Client.

As she studied the items on the white sheet, she chewed the tip of her pen. An image flashed through my mind of her full pink mouth and her breath mingling with mine. For an instant, I could taste the plumpness of her lips and feel the smooth skin of her chin brushing my jaw.

Where the hell had that come from? I'd never been anywhere near her mouth. Yet that flash had felt real, more like a memory than a fantasy. I shook the vision away. I'd encountered Violet occasionally since my bandmates of Full Throttle and I had begun working with Aidan, Violet's father and our band manager, but we hadn't talked much. I didn't remember her being this hot.

Though I found Violet undeniably beautiful, I'd never been actually attracted to her. Probably because she was all business and rarely smiled. She may as well have had a stamp on her forehead declaring her frigid. No way would I allow myself fantasies of kissing her, no matter how radiant she looked at this moment or how her curly red hair cascaded over her breasts.

Do not look at her breasts! Letting myself go in that direction would derail me from my goal after working so hard to get clean and sober. I didn't want another scandal, not when I needed to salvage my reputation, and I certainly couldn't risk a woman driving me back to drugs and booze.

I'd squeezed in a lifetime of brain-cell-killing substances these past three years. Countless women and too many mornings waking up with no memory of the night before. That had been my exact goal, no memory. I'd wanted to forget all the things I'd screwed up in my life, all the crappy people in my past, and the loved ones I'd lost.

In my quest to forget the pain, I'd totally failed myself in the process.

"If we're going to fix this kind of damage, I need your full attention. Don't check out on me." She peered up at me from her notes.

"I didn't check out." But I had. I'd been cruising down bad-memory lane. If I was going to get through this, I couldn't dwell on the past. I refocused on the here and now.

"Sebastian." Violet tapped a short, unpolished fingernail on my tabletop, then shoved her phone screen at me, displaying a picture — white powder on my nose, bleary half-closed eyes and my smile askew. "With hundreds, possibly thousands, more pictures just like this on the internet, we don't have time for distractions. I need all your energy focused on showing the world you've changed. You can't risk the record company refusing to promote you, or Liam not inviting you back into the band."

"Yeah, I know," I snapped. "My entire future is at stake. You don't have to remind me." Getting my life back would be a lot easier if my publicist was a little more pleasant to be around. If she fixed my rep though, she'd pull off a miracle. "You really think you can do that? I mean, not the daughter throwing part. You could make me look like a saint?"

"It's all in the presentation, the spin you put on it. Most people will believe just about anything," she muttered the last sentence, tossing her vibrant red hair off her shoulders.

I decided to ignore that last remark, which somehow felt personal. I barely knew Violet, so her attitude had to stem from something else in her life, her own baggage. Whatever. Either way, I'd give her the benefit of the doubt. She may have seemed distant at times, but I'd never known her to be openly rude.

"For some of the events, all you have to do is show up and smile for the camera. Maybe circulate around and be nice. The interviews will be a little trickier, but I'll coach you through those." She shivered and rubbed her bare arms.

I didn't think my house was chilly but she was wearing a tank top and she didn't look like she had enough meat on her bones to keep warm. I leaned way back, tipped my chair and slid the dining room window closed with a bang to shut out the chilly evening air.

"I've done plenty of interviews all by myself." God, I hated this. I wanted the next two months to be over already. "I can handle this on my own, V, but thanks."

"Sebastian, if you could handle everything on your own, I wouldn't be here, would I?" She stared at me, her eyes hard and cold. "And please don't call me V."

Her earlier dig couldn't have been my imagination. Apparently, compassion and optimism weren't qualities she inherited from Aidan. Not that the band's manager was always warm and fuzzy, but he knew when to snap out of business mode. "Fine, *Violet*, if you have me booked nearly full time trying to make myself look good, how will I have time to practice with Full Throttle for our upcoming CD?"

"You won't." She sighed. "You're not lead guitar anymore, remember? They'll record without you and after your reputation is cleaned up, you'll be back on tour with them. For now, your only job is to be seen as often as possible, doing good deeds so that enough positive things about you will bury the bad. Which means keeping current content on your social network pages, which hopefully will encourage the tabloids to stop running old photos from when you were a raging alcoholic."

No sugar coating, of course, not from Violet. Maybe the task would go down easier if she was a little more human about it. I was beginning to doubt that would happen. The sooner she was out of my house, the more at ease I'd be. I stood, the chair scraping the marble floor and toppling sideways. "Get out."

Violet flashed me a palm in a move of surrender. "Sorry, I didn't mean it that way. It's just that" — she blew out a frustrated breath — "we have a lot of damage control to do and it's going to take some work."

"Fine." I clenched my jaw. "Just keep the boozer comments to a minimum, huh?"

Her lips thinned and her gaze fell. "That was unprofessional and I apologize. It won't happen again," she said stiffly.

She couldn't even apologize properly. I wondered what I'd done so wrong. Or if some guy had walked all over her, broken her heart, and now she hated all of us. Twenty-two years old was awfully young to give up on all men.

Rumor had it that she'd avoided virtually all social interactions to get her marketing and public relations master's degree two years early. Probably hadn't been laid in ages. Maybe that was her problem — too much pent-up sexual frustration. Well, I certainly wouldn't be helping her out in that arena. I liked my women a little more agreeable.

Besides, I had a life to rebuild. I had no business chasing after any woman until I had my place back in the band. Right now, I had nothing to offer a girl. And once I was part of the band again, Violet would never make it on my list of potential girlfriends.

Unfortunately, I needed her help to accomplish all that. Our lead singer, Liam, had forced me out two months ago, and for that I'd be eternally grateful. Without his push, I wouldn't have confronted my very real problem. After thirty days in rehab, I'd shown up on his doorstep. He'd given me a fierce hug and told me I needed to *stay* clean. I also had to show the world I was truly on the right track before he invited me back.

I couldn't blame him. Prior to rehab, I was out of control. And Liam's fiancé had an impressionable four-year-old that he needed to set a good example for, as well as his three-year-old nephew. But, damn, I just wanted my bandmates back. I wanted my life back, my sense of normal. I found my passion through playing guitar and I wanted to do that with Full Throttle.

And Violet was my way to get that life back. I'd already learned the last four weeks that I couldn't do it on my own. I'd stayed out of trouble by house hunting, getting through escrow and moving. And in my spare time, I hit the gym. A lot. The adrenaline rush and exertion of energy kept me busy and motivated. But my mind was idle. And Liam didn't just want me to stop partying. He needed the world to know I was a good example of a human being.

My confidence in Violet's ability to salvage my rep was strong. I just needed to navigate around all her negativity. So I'd had a drinking problem, but I'd cleaned up and was in no danger of driving drunk and killing anyone. Just the very thought of all the things that could've happened in the constant stupor made me want to steer clear of alcohol forever. Thankfully, I didn't crave it anymore. My need to never again be oblivious overrode any thirst I might have.

Though I reveled in my ability to think clearly and my newfound awareness of my surroundings, I twitched at not being able to drown my problems in booze. For once in my life, I'd have to face my demons. But first thing was first. Right now, I had to concentrate on making Liam happy. Which brought me back around to Violet. We'd already been at it over an hour and the last couple of minutes, she'd been rattling off my agenda for the next week. I wanted to be done for the day.

I pointed at the pieces of paper in her hands and she lowered them to the table. "Are we finished yet?" I asked.

She tilted her head, her mouth twisting into a smirk. "Sorry, no."

"It's after ten and I need my beauty rest," I told her in a deadpan tone, rising from my chair to stand.

She flipped through the first couple sheets of paper, then plucked one up and studied the handwritten notes. "We have a few things we need to get started on right away."

I groaned, just wanting to get her and her attitude out of my house. "Can't it wait until tomorrow?"

"Depends." Violet lifted one brow and gave me a pointed look. "Can your career wait?"

I wondered if I should hire someone else to fix my reputation. But I knew Violet. She was hardcore. She'd made Liam's problems disappear and she was already familiar with how we worked. Not to mention, she'd already invested time into creating a plan to clean up my image, and lined up publicity appearances. Starting over with someone else would burn too much time.

I returned to the chair and glared at her. "Let's get this over with."

"Nothing would please me more," she said in an overly chipper tone as she hitched an index finger at her bulleted list. "You've got over a million followers on Twitter, even more on Instagram. I'd suggest using Facebook as well since you can go live and no one can accuse you of faking anything. You need content going out as much as possible throughout the day. Every post or video needs to show your sobriety, maturity, and stability. I've created a few temporary posts to go out steadily over the next few hours until you're able to post as you go."

My jaw went slack. "I can't waste time on social media all day." I could think of so many better things to do, like work on melodies for some lyrics.

Her eyes widened in mock innocence. "Oh, because you're so busy right now?"

What the hell was with her? She'd always been a bit aloof in the past, maybe even stuck up. But she'd never gone in for the kill. I hadn't seen her since... well, since her dad Aidan had sent her over to my house to check on me after Liam kicked me out of the band. Being the band's manager, he wanted to make sure I was okay. I had invited her inside and offered her a beer.

We'd had some drinks together and even laughed. We'd compared notes on our dads; hers who never stopped working and mine who never stopped drinking. I'd woken the next morning to an empty house and then I'd started off my day with another beer. Business as usual. So what did I do to piss her off?

Rather than rise to Violet's bait, I stood again in hopes that she'd take the hint. "I'm sure I'll be hearing from you if my posts don't meet your approval."

She turned to grab her jacket off the back of the chair, which I fervently hoped meant she was finally leaving, then she gathered the stack of papers. "If you use the premade posts, we won't have a problem."

"Right." I didn't care if she bossed me around or how condescending she was. At this point, I just wanted her gone. I led the way to the front door, praying on all that was holy that she was following me. As I glanced over my shoulder to check, I slowed and she bumped into me.

A vivid image of her bare stomach assaulted me and I flinched. I'd never had such crystal-clear fantasies about any woman who I hadn't slept with. Maybe I'd just gone too long without getting laid. I couldn't even remember the last time. Girls had been taking a back seat since my sister disappeared and alcohol had become my best friend and lover.

But I needed to worry about tomorrow, not yesterday.

"I'll be back in the morning to drive you to your AA meeting." Violet moved passed me toward the door.

"Whatever." I flung the door open and a burst of December air hit my neck, sending goose bumps over my skin. Much to my joy, she slipped right out and into her Lexus. Good riddance.

Too bad I'd be seeing her most every day for the next week. Minimally. My stomach filled with dread. Not only would her bad vibes be keeping me company — as if I really needed that in my life right now — but I'd be exposing my true self to the world. Sober. I hadn't done that in years. Would my fans like the real me? Hell, I wasn't even sure anymore who my true self was.

CHAPTER TWO
★ Violet ★

Frustrated tears burned my eyes as I tore out of Sebastian's driveway and through the gate. My expectations were low with Sebastian and I'd certainly never expected him to pursue me. I wasn't his type. For starters, I had more than half a brain. Every girl he'd been photographed with had big boobs, hair color from a bottle and fake eyelashes. Not that any of those things were necessarily evil. I just didn't have any of them. Didn't matter because he was nowhere near *my* type.

Well, ok, maybe a little my type. I could get lost in his beautiful soft brown eyes, or that thick wavy hair that made you want to run your hands through it, his wide mouth that smiled and disarmed you, the perfectly sculpted nose, his angular jaw and that incredible body.

How could he act as if nothing had happened between us? His obliviousness was downright offensive. The least he could do was pretend he'd had a good time. *Any* reaction would've been sufficient. Instead, since the moment he'd asked for a meeting with me, he'd behaved like a near stranger. To top it off, he had the nerve to be nice to me.

Over the years, people had called me cold, unfriendly and even indifferent, and I may have been those things to some people. But my small circle of loved ones were showered in affection. In business, I was professional. But above all, I didn't pretend to be someone I wasn't. I didn't pretend things didn't happen when they really did.

Two months ago, right after the band had dumped him, Sebastian called my dad in a rage. My dad was out of town and couldn't do anything to console him. He was also afraid Sebastian might do something stupid and make everything worse, so he asked me to drop by and check on him. When I arrived, Sebastian stumbled away, leaving the door wide open.

"Hey, beautiful," he slurred. As soon as he located his keys, he headed toward the door, tripping over a glass bowl. "Make yourself at home. I'll be back before you know it."

I stepped inside to see his furniture had been broken, shoebox-size holes decorated the walls and litter covered the floor. As much as I wished to be anywhere else at that moment, I couldn't walk away and let him drive his car. I had to distract him. "Want to hook me up with a drink before you rush out?"

"Sure, babe." He grinned, then staggered to a shelf and dropped his keys. As soon as he disappeared into the kitchen, I snagged the keys and closed the front door. The last thing I wanted to do was spend my evening with a drunk guy. But my dad had always liked Sebastian and I didn't want my dad to worry. I'd stay and make sure Sebastian didn't sober up and then get mad enough to go after Liam. Or do something even more insane.

Drink in hand, he offered me a seat. Since I hadn't been properly socialized growing up, I didn't know what to say to Sebastian or what to talk about. So I downed the beer and asked him questions about what inspired him to write lyrics and how he laid down the music. Surprisingly, his answers fascinated me, which led to more questions — and several more drinks.

Though he was wasted and I knew I wasn't talking to the real Sebastian, I got lost in conversation and then soon, I was almost as wasted as him. His hair had looked like it hadn't been cut in weeks and by the length of his beard, he hadn't shaved in even longer. Yet somehow, I'd let his gorgeous face and sexy smile momentarily blind me to the fact that he was a total loser. And I had ended up in bed with him.

Much to my horror the next morning, he lay deliciously naked, sprawled across his bed with his arm slung over my bare stomach. I carefully slipped out of his grasp, then plucked my panties from the overhead fan and retrieved my bra from the window sill. After a quick search through the trashed living room, I moved on to the kitchen where I spotted my jeans on the floor. Backtracking, I spied my shirt dangling on the staircase rail and quickly got dressed. I tiptoed out of his house and dashed down the long driveway. Once in my car, I sped away, nearly peeling out down the street.

I'd boozed-and-used with some guy who probably hadn't even graduated high school. I had never expected him to call me, nor had I wanted him to. And once I'd left his house, I had no intention of contacting him. I had plans for myself, a real future with stability that didn't include a troubled rock star with an uphill battle to have any kind of real future. But even if a guy doesn't send a girl flowers after a one-nighter, he could at least pretend like he had a good time, rather than behaving as though she were a stranger. We'd been naked together, for crying out loud. Yet he'd brushed me off this evening, as if that night two months ago had meant less than nothing to him.

I couldn't think of anything in my life I regretted more than having that first drink with Sebastian.

Though his behavior still irked me, hooking up with some tool wouldn't matter in the grand scheme of things. I would still dazzle the public with my media expertise and gather enough clients over the next three years to support myself. I'd meet a successful businessman — who wasn't an actor or musician — get married about two years later, and have my first child in time to have exactly three children total before I turned thirty.

I couldn't allow Sebastian's attitude to faze me. He wasn't worth the aggravation and his opinion didn't matter.

I wiped my wet cheeks and pulled into the driveway of my dad's house. Inside, I hung my keys on the hall tree by the door. I intended to rest just a moment before searching for my dad and saying hi, then slipping out the back door to the guest house. But once I dropped onto my dad's sofa, my limbs melted into the leather and I let my head fall back against the couch. I didn't want to move. Ever.

Why was I so exhausted? I slid sideways, curled my knees up and rested my cheek on the armrest.

I woke nine hours later with blinding light blazing through the open curtains and searing my brain. I flung off the throw blanket my dad had covered me with during the night and sprinted to the bathroom. Making it to the toilet just in time, my knees dropped to the Italian tile and I heaved.

And then I endured yet another spell of gagging and retching before my stomach had finally finished violating my self-esteem.

I wondered if I had eaten something bad the day before. Or maybe the stress and aggravation of being around Sebastian had brought back my old stomach issues. I'd probably be back to normal soon enough.

I stumbled on wobbly legs out the back door to the guest house to take a shower.

Dressed and ready to go, I shuffled back to the main house and stopped in my dad's office doorway. "Hey, Dad. On my way to meet up with Sebastian."

"Hi, sweetheart." He peered at me over his reading glasses. "Stomach acting up again?"

He'd heard me vomiting earlier, but he also knew I'd always had a nervous stomach and been prone to throwing up under extreme stress. But it had never been this bad. Three days in a row, I'd kept very little down. "I'll be fine. It's getting a bit better," I lied.

"You sure?" He shoved a stack of papers aside and rose from his desk. "You look a little pale. I can do all the rounds with Sebastian today, if you like."

"I need to do my job and you have plenty of your own work. Besides, you're a terrible photographer," I teased, trying to lighten the mood. "I need pictures with a high enough quality to leave no doubt it's Sebastian."

My dad nodded, studying me a beat, then he hesitantly lowered back into his seat. "All right. But if you don't get some color soon, I'd like you to consider seeing a doctor."

"Okay. Gotta go." I gave him a quick wave and dragged myself out of the house. Sometimes saying goodbye to my father was still awkward. My mom had disappeared with me when I was just a baby and I hadn't met him until she'd passed away when I was twelve. Though I thought the world of him and was grateful to still have one parent, after living with him ten years, I still couldn't quite warm up to him all the way. Maybe if he was less of a workaholic, we would've had more time to sort out the weirdness. Maybe if I was less obsessed with making something of myself, he would've had the opportunity to be a real father.

I slipped behind the wheel of my car, my mind coming up with all kinds of things I'd rather do than spend time with Sebastian. Disgust swirled in my stomach at the reminder that my entire day would be wasted on him. I almost wanted to hurl again, so I sucked in deep breaths and exhaled until the queasiness subsided.

After spending an hour on congested roads to travel ten miles, I steered my car to his gate, punched in the code he'd given me and, moments later, knocked on the front door. He opened it and raked his eyes over me, his mouth curved up as he spotted my jeans and boots. "I like that look on you."

Oh, *now* he was going to be nice and notice me? Nope, too late for that. I sighed and rolled my eyes.

He leaned against the doorframe, scowling. "What's your problem?"

"*My* problem?" My fingertips flew defensively to my chest. "I'm not the one with the problem."

Sebastian gave me a slow nod. "I disagree."

Said the guy who still hadn't invited me inside, despite the cold winds whipping my hair around my face. My chin lifted and I straightened my spine. "We can discuss this all morning while I freeze my ass off and we'd still get nowhere. Or you could get into my car so we make it to your nine o'clock meeting." I whirled and headed back down the driveway to my Lexus.

Bitch mode had been cranked up to the high setting. And I was pretty sure he was completely baffled. Just because he was thoroughly unaware of which totally inconsiderate act pissed me off didn't absolve him of the wrongdoing. And if he didn't want to feel a woman's wrath after sleeping with her, he should have the sense to follow after-sex protocol, starting with not behaving as if it never happened. Most guys at least put in effort to make the woman feel like their time together had meant something, especially if they moved in the same circles.

As soon as my butt touched the driver's seat and I was off my feet, my body turned to mush. Had I just not gotten enough sleep last night?

Sebastian jumped into the seat next to me — though I would have much rather he sit in the back like other dogs — and I took a deep breath, muscling through the lethargy. I had to be on my game. Sebastian needed his rep back and I needed my career on track for my eight-year plan. My success depended heavily on how I handled Sebastian and reshaped his image.

We drove to his meeting in dead silence. Not wanting anyone to think Sebastian and I were together, I waited in the car while he walked up to the plain stucco building where his AA meeting was held. I had originally planned to take him to a more upscale meeting in Beverly Hills, but decided the seedier side of Hollywood suited him better. Plus, this hole in the wall more than likely had regular people, the kind who wouldn't respect his privacy. I didn't want them to hold back like a fellow celebrity might. I wanted them to spill their pictures and posts all over social media.

Three respectable minutes later, I slipped inside the building and followed the signs to a spacious room with a stage. Judging by the medieval costume strewn over a chair and the three stools on stage, I guessed the room was used for acting classes or plays. I claimed a seat in the back. People had already recognized him — two guys flanked him, talking animatedly while a girl, probably not much older than me, was trying to get his attention by casually pacing back and forth in front of him.

I scanned the room again, spotting a skinny dude in the corner aiming his phone at Sebastian. Good, that would get on the internet quickly. As soon as I could take pictures without anyone noticing, I whipped out my own cell and, careful not to get caught, snapped a few of my own shots. I made sure only Sebastian entered the frame, since the meeting was supposed to be anonymous. Not that the other people aiming cameras at him cared about anyone's privacy.

Someone walked up to the podium and I slid my phone back into my purse, then sneaked out the back and into my car.

★

Tap! Tap! Tap!

My heavy lids scraped over my eyes and I squinted as the sun beat down on the windshield of my car. Using my long sleeve, I rubbed my chin to remove the drool.

Tap! Tap! Tap!

I snapped to my left and rolled the window down a crack.

"Are you going to let me in or not?" Sebastian scowled.

Where was I? A quick scan reminded me we were outside the AA meeting. I shook off the brain fog and unlocked the doors. As Sebastian climbed into the passenger side, I stalled to readjust my seat and rummage through my purse. Driving was not something I should do just yet, not until I woke up a bit more.

"Are you okay? Do you want me to drive?" Sebastian asked.

Feeling more alert by the second, I fired up the engine. "Nah, I got this."

"Where to now?" Sebastian rolled his window down and the nausea that had been percolating in my stomach eased up.

"Lunch, which we'll be doing together a lot. You need to be seen in public as much as possible. Hope you brought money." I pulled onto the street and headed toward the trendiest restaurant in Hollywood that boasted the most celebrity sightings. That's where the paparazzi would be searching for people like Sebastian. "We don't necessarily want to give anyone a reason to believe we're a couple. Be sure to keep your distance and try not to look at me too adoringly."

"I can't make any promises. You make yourself absolutely irresistible," he said dryly, following it up with a snort.

I allowed myself a small, amused smile and glanced away from him to check the left lane for my turn. By the time I faced ahead again, I'd regained my stony expression. "If anyone asks, you can say I'm your AA sponsor."

"Works for me."

Thankfully, the restaurant had valet parking, so my hot, swollen feet didn't have far to carry me. My feet were always the first part of me to feel the chill. Why weren't they cold like the rest of my body?

The hostess seated us at a corner booth with one long seat and I grumbled to myself. I had hoped we'd be situated in the middle of the restaurant where everyone could see us. But it was nearly lunchtime and most tables were already taken.

The smell of beef wafted up my nose and saliva pooled in my mouth, but not in the good way. Normally, I liked beef, but not today. My entire body rebelled against the smell of the restaurant.

"Excuse me." I bolted from the booth and made tracks for the restroom. I skidded into the stall and moved my mass of hair out of the way just in time before I tossed up my breakfast. Whimpering, I rinsed my mouth from the faucet, then composed myself a moment before returning to the table.

"Are you okay?" Sebastian had the decency to look concerned, but since it was his fault my stress level had risen to epic heights, it was the least he could do. "You're whiter than usual."

"The meat smell in here is pretty strong." I snagged a menu and began looking for anything that might be remotely appetizing. "It's turning my stomach."

"I can see that." He scooted sideways in the booth until he was close enough to lay a hand across my forehead. "You don't feel hot, but I'm thinking maybe I should take you home anyway."

Home... I longed to crawl into bed and I didn't care that it was only lunchtime. I could sleep for a week. But then I'd lose a whole day where Sebastian could be rebuilding his image. Reshaping his future by massaging the media, thereby changing public opinion, was what I did best and what I had to do in order to accomplish my goals. Sebastian and this milestone would be one of many goals achieved toward the plan I'd carefully laid while I was still in high school.

A little stomach issue wasn't going to throw me off. Nothing would. I refused to ever let myself get anywhere near the level of poverty I'd grown up with. When my mom had left my dad, she'd disappeared with me and never looked back. But without him around to help out, we were too destitute to afford proper medical care. I vowed not to end up like her, dying in a hospital room because she'd been too busy working two jobs to take the time to get a checkup. If she had caught it in time, maybe they could have stopped the cancer before it was too late and she wouldn't have been ravaged by it. I refused to let that be my future. The only way I'd accomplish my goals was not to allow myself to get distracted. That started with men.

It wasn't just my ambition and determination that had me cringing over abandoning my job; I didn't want to let anyone down. I didn't want to disappoint my father. His livelihood depended on Full Throttle's success. "I really am fine. Just missed breakfast."

He shot me a skeptical look. "If you say so."

"I've always had a nervous stomach and it acts up when I'm stressed." I flashed him an irritated look. He shook his head and proceeded to ignore me until the waiter came by to take our order.

With great effort, I managed to choke down some pasta and garlic bread. Years of nausea had taught me to stick with breads and grains to settle the stomach. It helped, but this degree of discomfort baffled me. My stomach issues had never been this bad. I'd thrown up twice between yesterday and today, and I still felt like crap. Obviously this wasn't a twenty-four hour bug. I probably had some kind of virus.

My dad's words nagged at me. But if it didn't improve soon, no one would have to drag me to the doctor. I hated feeling poorly, and vomiting was one of the worst things to experience. Truly disgusting.

And it sucked the energy right out of me.

My fork slipped from my fingers and clattered to the plate. "I could be contagious. I really hope you don't catch this. I'm not even sure I should be out in public." I slumped. "This is going to set us back."

"It doesn't have to. I can go home and get on Twitter for a while. Maybe work on some lyrics while I'm live on Facebook. That could keep me busy for hours and everyone will be able to see I'm not drinking. You can go home and rest guilt free."

Maybe Sebastian wasn't as inconsiderate as I'd thought. I practically moaned in relief. "Gladly."

He flagged down our waiter for the check and several minutes later, we were standing at the driver's side of my Lexus. He held out his palm. "Key?"

I rarely let anyone use my car. But the idea of driving seemed daunting and if I were to be honest with myself, my reflexes weren't exactly at their best. I let Sebastian take the wheel, grateful I could sink into the passenger seat and close my eyes.

Seconds later, the car stopped and I wondered if Sebastian had encountered a problem. Then I focused on my house only yards away. Geez, had we teleported or something?

"Did you have a nice nap?" Sebastian asked, killing the engine and handing me the keys.

Considering I hadn't even realized I'd been sleeping, yes. But he didn't need to know how comatose I'd been. "Shouldn't I drop you off at home?"

"No need. Theo lives a few blocks from here and walking will get me moving since I missed my workout this morning. I'll drop in on Theo, maybe snag one of his cars. Or I can take a Lyft or Uber." He exited and was already around to my side by the time I grabbed my purse. He opened the passenger door and peered down at me. "Sure you're okay?"

I nodded, trying not to visualize him lifting weights at Theo's. He'd bulked up over the last couple months and I couldn't help but wonder if his muscles would feel differently against me.

Flinching, I pushed those thoughts away. My attraction to him was purely physical and I wanted so much more from a relationship. I wanted an intelligent man who wasn't obsessed with his looks. Someone not in the spotlight with girls vying for his attention. I'd spent the last decade around musicians, seen how most of them operated. I didn't want that kind of life.

"Hey." Sebastian leaned in, getting a closer look at me. "You need me to go to the pharmacy or something? Or I can drive you to urgent care."

Wow, I really needed to focus and not get distracted by Sebastian or wonder what he had going on under his clothes, especially with him standing right in front of me. I probably looked like an idiot.

"Thank you, but I'm much better. Promise." The nausea had passed and I felt normal again, except for the fatigue.

"Good. When you get around to it, text me about tomorrow." He waved and strolled down the street toward Theo's.

My gaze magnetically zeroed in on his butt that had become much more firm and muscular since our night of debauchery. I blinked, disgusted with myself. Seriously, he was a gifted lyricist and received numerous accolades for his guitar skills, but being talented in one area didn't automatically make him a decent person. Talent and looks weren't enough for me. I spun and darted down the driveway to the guest house, kicked off my shoes and sprawled out on my bed. And not even the image of Sebastian's fine ass could keep me awake.

CHAPTER THREE
★ Sebastian ★

Throughout my entire exercise routine the next morning, my thoughts kept drifting to Violet. I could totally see how her stress levels might skyrocket from being so uptight all the time. That girl needed to relax in a big way, let her hair down.

A flash of her straddling my hips, the ends of her red curls tickling my face while we laughed, assaulted me. I dropped from the salmon ladder, then wiped my chest and neck with a towel. Why the hell couldn't I get Violet out of my head? She had no business being there. And, seriously, if I got together with any woman, it wouldn't be with someone so high-strung that she developed physical reactions. Hell, I didn't need the extra stress in my life.

One thing I'd never learned to swallow was cutting toxic people from my life. It had taken me forever to do that with my parents, who were the most poisonous of them all. Though I never saw or spoke to them anymore, I still wondered where they were and what they were doing. And if there was any hope for them. Did my mom still justify her and my dad's drinking and hold him above everyone else, even over her own kids? Always coming in last hadn't been the worst thing, but leaving my sister, India, behind had nearly killed me. She'd been seven years younger than me and she couldn't defend herself against our dad's verbal or physical abuse.

An ache began in my throat at the memory of her. She was fifteen when I'd last seen her three years ago. She'd just disappeared without a word and I didn't know whether she was dead or alive. I rubbed my chest remembering the detective's last words, that they needed to put their manpower toward children they might actually find. They promised to keep searching when they could, but the chances of her being alive were slim.

My jaw hurt from clenching it and I moved it from side to side to relax. I pushed the image of India's face out of my head and stepped onto the treadmill. If only I'd done something to help her, found a way to get her out of that house. Instead, I'd left her there to fend for herself. And then she'd run away. Or been abducted. Or worse. I'd hired two private investigators over the last three years and they had come up with squat.

But I couldn't go there. I'd never forget India, but I couldn't keep revisiting her fate, whatever it had been. Thinking of her and all the ways she could've suffered would only bury me and I couldn't afford to go back to drowning my regrets in a bottle. I needed to stay with the living and concentrate on my future, maybe even enter a real relationship once I was back in the band.

And once again, Violet's face swam before me. She wasn't a relationship prospect for me. Now or ever. I set the treadmill speed faster, hoping the exertion would distract me. By the time I finished my usual four miles, I'd had sex with Violet in my head six times. Filled with self-loathing, I nabbed a pencil and paper, and made a beeline for my guitar. Working on lyrics always soothed my soul and playing guitar healed me. Maybe I could return to normal and get Violet's image out of my head before she arrived in less than a half hour.

My feelings for you, how my love raged. All for you, the wars I have waged. But no battles were fought, and I left you behind. Now I'm drowning in guilt, I'm losing my mind.

I hummed, then rolled the lyrics over the melody as I played. That wasn't right. I started in a different chord and sang the first line again, this time a little raspier to match the unsettling lyrics. Then I tossed aside the guitar and scribbled a flood of words, filling the sheet. After making a few more tweaks, I picked up my guitar again, and experimented with a slightly different melody. Yeah, that worked for me.

I sang through the second verse. "Your love filled me and gave me speed. How could I know you'd make me bleed? Now you're gone and I'm all alone, to deal with the seeds that I have sown." I dived right into the chorus. "Tell me the rage will go away, that I'll live to fight another day." I did a short guitar solo, then rolled into the bridge. "Falling fast, I'm nearly destroyed. Make it stop, send me into the void."

Yeah, that's what I'd been needing. All the tension that had been slowly suffocating me had gradually seeped out during the songwriting process, like I'd been cleansed of all the bad things in my life.

"Uhm..." Violet cleared her throat. "I hate to interrupt. You seem so happy. But if we don't leave soon, we're going to be late for the interview, unless we skip lunch. I don't want you to miss out on the chance to be seen. And you still need to put on a shirt."

I glanced up at Violet and my shoulders tensed. There went all the tranquility I'd just created. Some warning would have been nice. Maybe I shouldn't have given her the code to my front gate. And what the hell was she wearing? Could anyone really call that a skirt? Wasn't she cold? Maybe she was banking on the leather jacket keeping her legs warm. "How did you get in?"

She shifted uncomfortably, her fingers clasped tightly around a key. "Sorry. When you didn't answer your door, I got worried and called my dad. He told me where you keep the extra key."

"Lost track of time and didn't hear you knock." Damn, she looked amazing. "Give me five minutes while I get showered and dressed." And I would try not to think about that V-neck that showed just enough of her breasts to make me wonder what they'd feel like in my hands. Or in my mouth.

Damn it. I bolted into my bedroom, chastising myself for the direction of my thoughts.

Violet was high-maintenance and rude. She wasn't for me and she never would be. I kept reminding myself of that as I showered, then threw on jeans and a black, button-down shirt. On my way out of my room, I scooped up my military boots and rushed back to Violet. She was sitting on the sofa scanning my lyrics.

"That's not finished yet." I ran a hand through my wet hair, not sure I wanted an outsider, especially Violet, to see my stuff before I passed it by one of my bandmates.

"It's amazing." She glanced up from the sheet, her lashes wet. "You must have loved her very much to transfer that much raw emotion into a song."

Okay, maybe I didn't mind Violet reading it. But no way would I discuss my sister with the queen of cold. I shrugged. "You ready?" Without waiting for a reply, I made tracks for the garage.

"I guess you're driving," she said, stopping in front of my shiny red convertible Bugatti. "How'd you get this anyway? I thought this was the number one most expensive car ever."

"Got a good deal on it, because some rapper guy couldn't keep it under one-fifty. His girl thought he was going to get himself killed in a high-speed car chase. Made him get rid of it." I opened the door for her. "For a really sweet price."

"It'll certainly get us some attention." She slipped into the passenger seat. "Which is the whole point."

Between the car and her short skirt, we'd probably accomplish everything we wanted to today and more. I reached into the console to get the garage door opener, brushing her arm in the process. Ignoring the tingle on my skin and blaming it on my lack of contact with women these last three years, I concentrated on the future. I was about to spend the day with one of the most beautiful girls I'd encountered in forever. May as well enjoy it.

On second thought, that probably wasn't possible with a girl like Violet.

"If we're going to make the headlines, let's make sure we're seen." I removed the top of the Bugatti, then we climbed in. After firing it up, I cleared the garage door, passed the gate and pulled onto the street.

Violet gathered her massive amounts of hair and wound it into a ball, then held it in place with an elastic tie. I liked how she was prepared for anything. Rather than getting turned off by her practicality, I was aroused by it. But hadn't I already concluded that my attraction to her was because I'd been too long without a woman? My appendages were simply responding to lack of activity. That's all there was to it.

"They'll assume we're an item. Is that going to bother you?" I asked her.

"I couldn't care less so long as we both get what we want. Besides, people love a good romance. They love a mystery even more. While the paparazzi are speculating, you'll be getting exposure."

Wow, what I had started to view as a joy ride, Violet had managed to turn back into a business transaction. I knew I was just a problem for her to solve and she was only doing her job. But, for some reason, having so little value to her made me feel a little more hollow inside. And, apparently, sobering up had turned me into a wuss.

CHAPTER FOUR
★ *Violet* ★

When I'd walked into Sebastian's living room a few minutes ago, and saw him singing as he strummed his Fender, my stomach had flipped. Over the last couple of months, he'd become perfectly sculpted, unlike the softer man I'd gotten drunk with. His hair had been damp and the sparse hairs along his happy trail had glistened over solid muscle. He'd obviously recently finished a workout and I was thankful to have missed it or I might have fainted.

He was fully clothed now and I wasn't drunk. And, thankfully, I'd been such a hag to him there was no way in hell he could be even remotely interested in me. I couldn't imagine him going for a boring businesswoman when he could sleaze it up with some heiress or starlet. Nothing else would happen between us. I would keep my lust in check and I'd get through this job in no time.

"How are you feeling today?" Sebastian's gaze flicked my way a moment before steering the Bugatti onto Sunset Boulevard.

"Decent." Not entirely true. Though I probably wasn't in any danger of puking up my guts, being with Sebastian seemed to up my anxiety level. He was a douche bag and too gorgeous for his own good. Or mine. But as long as he kept that shirt on, at least his looks wouldn't throw me off my game. Much.

Screams on the opposite side of the street were followed by shouts in our direction. "Sebastian Trevino! Oh, my God, it's Sebastian! It's him!"

I glanced straight ahead to the red light, then refocused on the girls. They were weaving through sidewalk body traffic and sprinting in our direction. "Sebastian, wait!" a tiny blonde begged.

Sebastian laughed. "We're parking in a moment and we'll come back to say hello." The girls shrieked in unison and he hit the gas. "Do we have time?" he asked me.

"We don't have a choice now that you've promised them." He was about to willingly brave a group of screaming fans. He had to be crazy. But whatever. It was his career. I could lead him to the right choice, but I couldn't make the decision for him. I just didn't want him screwing up my hard work by being late to the interview, because he had to suck up to his fans. "Let's be quick about it."

Sebastian swerved and slipped into a parking spot on the street. We had to walk a block to get to the girls, which wasn't an outrageously long distance by any stretch of the imagination. But it would burn time. I'd worked hard to line up the interview on such short notice with *Exposed!* magazine. Normally, they'd send someone out to the celebrity's house, but Sebastian had only recently closed escrow and moved in. He'd seen the paparazzi go after Liam and he wasn't ready to have his property invaded yet. I figured getting out into the world and being seen would help the mission anyway. As long as we were on time.

The girls greeted us halfway from the shop where we'd first seen them. The blonde jumped up and down while another girl stood dumbstruck, and the third one wrung her hands, grinning at Sebastian like she worshipped him.

Blondie squealed and thrust a napkin and pen toward Sebastian. "Do you think you could sign this?"

He flashed the most gorgeous smile I'd ever seen as he took the pen and napkin. "What's your name, doll?"

I caught myself melting and reminded myself I didn't date musicians, especially loser alcoholics who didn't even have a job.

"Would you like to take a picture with me?" he

asked them, returning the signed napkin.

After a few shots with the girls, I urged Sebastian to leave and we rushed to make it to the interview. He and I made it to the *Exposed!* building with only seconds to spare. We rushed up the elevator and as soon as the receptionist recognized him, we were escorted to a private room. We crossed the fake wood floors and each sunk into an overstuffed chair. So that I wouldn't have to talk to Sebastian, I grabbed the current issue of *Exposed!* off the side table.

But I couldn't concentrate on any celebrity tidbits. I was too busy remembering how sweet Sebastian had been to the girls and the looks on their faces when he hugged them. I scolded myself for the warm and fuzzies creeping up on me.

We didn't have long to wait before a woman entered. She wore a snug pencil skirt and a white blouse that dipped low in the front. Her lipstick was painted just above her lip line which made her mouth appear fuller. But the bright red also reminded me of the Joker. Other than that, she could be pretty, I supposed. If you liked red hair that came from a bottle.

"Hi, I'm Lisa Alcott." She bent forward to extend a hand to Sebastian, her boobs nearly toppling out and falling on him. She held his fingers much longer than necessary.

Despite being repelled by her insincerity, I

plastered on a smile, ready to introduce myself as the one she'd spoken with when setting up the meeting. She didn't even glance in my direction. My hackles went up when I realized she didn't plan to acknowledge my existence in any way.

"Let's get right to it, shall we?" she asked, oozing something that was more like smarm than charm.

I inwardly twitched, wondering if Sebastian found her attractive. But if he liked plastic women and wanted to hook up with a piranha, that was his business.

Sebastian flashed that brilliant smile and I relaxed. He wouldn't fall for her act. He was working her better than she was working him.

God, I hated Hollywood.

"So..." She gave him angelic eyes and her sweetest smile. "Let's talk about your sister's disappearance."

His sister? My eyes cut to Sebastian's stricken face. Clearly, Lisa had hit a chord and who could blame him for being stunned? I didn't know Sebastian even had a sister, much less that something had happened to her. But now wasn't the time to get my curiosity satisfied. Sebastian needed rescuing and the whole reason I'd come to the meeting was to make sure it turned out beneficial to him. "We're limiting the interview to Full Throttle's upcoming CD. Sebastian has also agreed to take questions on his newfound sobriety, but any other questions, he'll have no comment."

Sebastian shook his head and sent me a reassuring smile. "It's okay." Then he turned to Lisa. "Old news, but if you want to recycle something from three years ago, be my guest. What would you like to know?"

"Have they come up with any new evidence in the case?"

"Not that I know of. We've barely heard from anyone at the police station in probably two years."

She scribbled on the notepad in her lap, then peered up at Sebastian. "And your parents? How are they doing?"

A slow smile crept over his face. "You already know all this. What's your angle?"

Her eyes widened in feigned innocence. "Responsible journalism?"

I snorted and she sent me a death glare. "Whatever you really want to know, just ask. If he doesn't want to answer, he won't. But let's not waste everyone's time."

Lisa pivoted in her seat and stared straight at me. "I'm afraid I'm going to have to ask you to leave. We reserve the right to conduct interviews without an audience." She rose to open the door, but Sebastian's voice had her halting midstep.

"She stays or I leave." He waved her back to the chair. "Next question?"

"Very well." Resigned, Lisa huffed and returned to her seat, crossed her legs and reviewed her list. "Were you aware that after your father passed away, your mother became unstable and was admitted to a hospital two weeks ago where she remains in a coma?"

He folded his arms over his chest and dipped his head to the side. "Next question."

She lowered her chin and straightened her spine. "Do you want to know which hospital she's at?"

Sebastian checked his phone, eyeing the screen. "If you have any *real* questions, I suggest you get to it. We have somewhere across town we need to be."

Lisa's face fell and she cleared her throat, as if Sebastian had finally broken her. "Are you dating anyone?" she asked.

"Not right now."

"You haven't been photographed with a woman in some time and your Full Throttle fans are anxious to know if you're straight."

He laughed, a beautiful robust sound I found incredibly sexy. "Women are definitely my drug of choice."

The rest of the questions went off smoothly and Sebastian answered all of them without needing any further assistance from me. Not that he had needed me at all. After the last question, Lisa laid on the sugar and told Sebastian how lovely it had been to meet him. Then she ushered us out. We walked at a casual pace until we were safely tucked inside the Bugatti. The energy around him changed as he put up the top and closed us in. His fingers trembled as he started the car. "I need to get to the hospital."

His sudden rush to see his mom had to mean that he hadn't known anything about her current state. "Of course."

"Let's get you something to eat first." He twisted around so he could back the car out of the spot.

"No, it's okay. You need to see your mother. I can take an Uber back to your house or something." But I dreaded that option. Not only did I not want to spend the money on a ride, but I'd still have to get home from his house. By the time I got home, I would've probably fainted from hunger. I really didn't want to skip a meal and be twice as queasy later.

He braked and faced me. "I'm going to feed you. Then I'm going get you back to your car. No arguments."

Five minutes in traffic on our way to The Bass, I couldn't hold back my curiosity. "How long since you've seen your parents?"

His breath rushed out. "Over three years."

I mulled over that new information. "You had no idea your dad passed away? No one told you?"

Sebastian's long fingers stretched out, then

tightened around the steering wheel as he stared straight ahead. "No. My parents kept to themselves and never mentioned other family. They burned a lot of bridges with friends, and even if their neighbors knew, they probably assumed I found out through someone else."

I let the silence engulf us the rest of the way to the restaurant, thinking he probably needed some time to digest the fact that his dad died. Did he feel guilty for not being there for his dad? He must've had a falling out with his parents for them to be estranged. And now his mom was in a coma. My chest tightened for Sebastian and everything he had to be feeling.

After parking at the curb right in front of The Bass, Sebastian dropped his keys in the palm of the valet, took the ticket and we made our way to the restaurant entrance. He opened the door for me and his fingertips found my lower back as I brushed past him. A tiny chill shimmied up my spine.

Once seated, he studied his menu a few heartbeats, then set it down and leaned over the table, his voice low. "Why wouldn't the hospital or someone contact me when my mother was admitted?"

I tilted my head and pursed my lips as I contemplated the answer. Taking the hint that he didn't want our conversation overhead, I rested my elbows on the table and huddled with him. "Wouldn't your parents have final say on who is notified, and what information is released to whom, if anything happened to one of them?"

"Dumb question. I don't know why I asked."

"I take it that you and your parents parted on bad terms." I hoped he'd volunteer to fill in the blanks for me.

"After a huge fight, they vowed I was dead to them." He hung his head, hands fisting. "Then things got uglier. They wouldn't even let me see my sister. By the time I got the paperwork started to get custody of India, it was too late. She'd disappeared."

"I'm so sorry." I almost reached out for his hand to comfort him, but then remembered I didn't like him.

A flash lit up our corner and I glanced toward the light. Paparazzi. Which was exactly what I'd been hoping for. Except that Sebastian and I looked like we were having an intimate conversation. Plus, this was a very personal moment for Sebastian, which shouldn't have been intruded on.

"Like you said, people love to speculate." He straightened, moving away from me. "They'll have fun with that photo."

"Yep." The photographer would probably try to follow Sebastian to the hospital, get all up in his business. Under normal circumstances, paparazzi wouldn't bother me. But Sebastian had just learned his dad had passed and his mom was in a coma. He didn't need the media prying right now, not into his family life. I leaned toward Sebastian and whispered, "Why don't I go to the hospital with you? Maybe I could deflect some of that BS while you do what you need to do. If we run into any paparazzi, I could say that I have a doctor's appointment or something."

He nodded slowly, his eyes narrowed as though he were deep in thought. "I hate to do that to you, but you'd probably be saving my ass."

And sacrificing my own. Working was one thing. Helping him deal with his parents would only soften me up toward him and increase the chances of me getting sucked in by that pretty face. After tonight, I'd keep it strictly business. If he needed help, too bad. He was on his own.

CHAPTER FIVE
★ *Sebastian* ★

I'd lost the paparazzi miles before reaching the hospital, but I didn't tell Violet. Guilt crept up on me for dragging her along when she could have been working on something else. But I wanted company for this mission and, for some reason I couldn't fathom, I wanted that company to be Violet. Her of all people, what the hell? I had no business associating with her for things not related to my career or my image.

I crossed my mental fingers that my parents hadn't moved and switched doctors. If they had, I'd have to do some footwork to find her. Maybe I'd get lucky and my mom would be at the first hospital I checked, and less of Violet's time would be wasted.

We waited at the counter on the first floor while three nurses bustled on the other side, all of them appearing too busy to assist us. Seconds stretched and I tapped the counter impatiently. A brunette who looked barely legal darted a glance my way, then did a double take. She blinked and almost lost her grasp on a stack of files. Well, good. If she recognized me, maybe I'd get faster service. I wasn't above using my fame for my own purposes for something important, like quickly finding my comatose mother.

"Hi." I flashed her a smile, one I hoped would dazzle her into being my slave. "I'm looking for my mother, Valentina Trevino. Can you tell me what room she's in?"

"Uhm." Her face still frozen, she set the files on a cabinet nearby and punched a few buttons on a keyboard. It didn't escape my notice that she didn't ask how to spell my last name. She already knew. She studied the monitor, then peered over at me. "She's upstairs in Neurology, sixth floor."

"Thanks so much." I jerked my head toward the elevator and Violet followed me. Just a few floors up and I'd see my mom. But did I actually want to be in the same room with her? God, what if she woke up while I was there? The elevator doors swished shut and the floor beneath us moved. I wiped my sweaty palms on my jeans.

Violet's sympathetic eyes regarded me. "Are you okay?"

I offered her a small smile. "Haven't decided yet."

"Do you want me to leave?" she asked in a gentle voice. "No signs of paparazzi. You're probably safe."

Hell, no, I didn't want her to go. Not when she looked at me like that, all sweet and soft. I had this urge to stop the elevator and trap her in there with me for at least twenty-four hours. How could I get her to stay? "Uh..."

"It's okay." The elevator dinged and her eyes darted to the door. "Let's find your mom."

Gratitude filled me. Along with something else, not unlike affection. The doors opened and I extended an arm to urge her out. She paused in front of the elevator, not sure which way to go and I used that excuse to touch her, my fingertips lightly grazing her hip. I let them skim along her body and land on her elbow. Making contact with her arm was far less obvious than her lower back, but I still got to satisfy my curiosity while not looking like a total pervert.

But curiosity and physical attraction were a far cry from real affection. I wasn't too worried about becoming attached to Violet. Sooner or later, she'd say something rude or insensitive and obliterate any affinity I may have developed for her. For now, I just needed her to help me through the next few minutes.

We stopped at the nurses' station, a long low counter protected by glass that separated us from them. The male nurse in front of me glanced up. "Can I help you?"

"I'm looking for my mother, Valentina Trevino. Can you tell me what room she's in?"

He flipped through a binder, his index finger following the line of the column. He stopped at room 607 and there was my mother's name. "And you are?"

"SebastianTrevino. She's my mother." I'd already said that. Duh.

"Room 607. Around the corner and all the way down at the end. Be sure to check in with the nurses there to double check. Sometimes they get transferred or released and we don't find out right away."

I'd already begun walking, feeling adrenaline roar through me when I heard Violet answer, "Thank you." I could feel her close behind me, but anything outside the hammering in my ears faded away. We passed room 602 and I knew my mom's room was coming soon. The closer I grew to her, the narrower the corridor walls seemed. Images of her screaming swam before me. My skin remembered the sting of a paddle for coming into the kitchen.

I froze. Did I really want to see my mom? Would she bring me anything but pain?

"Excuse me, sir? Can I help you?"

I stared at the number 607, unable to move my feet.

"Sir?" the tiny, faraway voice asked.

"We're looking for Mrs. Trevino." Violet looped her arm through mine and I still didn't move. "But I think we'll need a moment before our visit with her."

"That won't be necessary. She was released this morning," a woman's voice replied. My emotions were still ping-ponging between relief that I wouldn't be seeing her today and disappointment that she still had the power to hurt me.

I sucked in air, filling my lungs to capacity, then let it out. I didn't like hospitals. They smelled weird. Cold and sterile. I itched to flee. But I needed to see this through.

"Can you tell us what happened?" Violet asked. I owed her big time.

"I'm afraid not. I can't release information without the patient's permission."

I dragged my gaze from the white walls to see a heavy woman wearing black-rimmed glasses and baby blue scrubs. "I need to know what happened to my mother and if she's okay."

Her eyes narrowed as if she was contemplating what to tell me. "Let me see if there's any information I can give you. Wait here." She shuffled around the nurse's station and disappeared through another door.

Violet released my arm and turned to face me. "How are you doing?"

"Not great. We'll stay for whatever she can give us, but then I'm calling it a day."

She tugged on my arm, pulling me toward the wall as an older man wearing a hospital gown approached. "We should get out of the way."

Of course we should. But my brain had begun to retard as soon as I'd stepped out of the elevator. I leaned against the cold wall, staring straight ahead while my brain cells came back to life, one by one.

Several minutes later, the female nurse returned and I snapped to attention. She opened the file and studied it a beat, her voice lowering to a whisper. "She was brought in for a drug overdose. Apparently, your mother had fallen and hit her head, which caused the brain to swell. She was given Propofol until the risk of further injury was reduced." She squinted her eyes at the paper. "Four days later, drugs were slowly decreased until she regained consciousness. Early this morning, she became verbally abusive and demanded to be released. Against doctor's recommendations, of course."

"Okay, so..." Violet looked like she was mulling over the information and I waited to see what she was going to say. Clearly, I wasn't going to do a damn thing. "Basically, she was probably going through withdrawals and being here wasn't getting her any closer to her next fix. You think that sums it up?"

She sighed, shaking her head. "Unfortunately, that's usually the way it goes."

"Thank you so much for your help." Violet smiled

at the nurse and jerked her head in the opposite direction. "Let's get you out of here."

"Great, my mom's no longer a heavy drinker like my dad was. She graduated to hard drugs dangerous enough to send her to a hospital." Now I wanted even less to do with her.

Violet tugged on my hand and I realized I'd been only inching along. I picked up my pace and entered the elevator with her.

"*She* chose that path, Sebastian. Every decision she made has led her to this place in life."

I nodded numbly, struggling to snap out of the brain fog I'd plummeted into. When we arrived at my car, I took the passenger side and let Violet drive the Bugatti, knowing I was too disturbed and still mentally wasted from the last couple of hours.

Violet exited the parking structure and turned onto the road toward my house. I stared out the window.

The little boy in me wished my mother could be saved. If I had stuck around, could I have prevented this? If I had reconnected with them once I'd become successful, could I have arranged help for them or somehow gotten them into rehab? If I had, would my dad be alive now?

Once the car was tucked away in my garage, Violet got out of the Bugatti and tossed me the keys. I unlocked the door that led to my house and walked straight to the living room. In my peripheral vision, Violet moved like a shadow as she crept toward the front door.

"Thanks for today. For everything. You didn't have to do all that."

She shrugged. "Write a song live on Facebook tonight. It'll make up for not being seen more today."

And back to business. She must have hated being forced to take care of me. Probably relieved to get away. I walked her to the front door and watched from the porch to ensure she got safely into the Lexus. She drove past the gate and I made sure it closed behind her, then I dialed my private investigator. He'd find out my dad's cause of death and he could probably locate my mom. Even if I didn't speak to her, I wanted to know where she was.

My PI's phone rang twice and I hit the end button, growling as I tossed my phone on the sofa. Maybe I didn't want to know what my mom was up to. She'd only reel me in again and I couldn't afford to let that kind of poison back into my life. I'd call the investigator again at some point, after I was part of Full Throttle again and back to normal. In the meantime, I needed something distracting to get me through the next few weeks. Which did not involve thinking of my parents. I switched on the

TV and flipped through the channels. When I came across a rerun of The Shawshank Redemption, I set down the remote, leaned into the back of the couch and escaped into a different world. When my lids drifted shut, I wasn't thinking about my dad or mom, or even my missing sister. I thought of long red locks and sparkling green eyes.

CHAPTER SIX
★ Violet ★

After a fitful night's sleep imagining Sebastian's hard biceps wrapped around me and his firm abdomen against mine, I rolled over and switched off my alarm clock. I mentally added another item to my Things to Avoid with Sebastian list. In addition to keeping his clothes on, he needed not to touch me. Or vice versa. Ever.

When that kind of crazy sexy comes into contact with any part of my body, my brain short circuits. I barely held it together at the hospital when I had to make skin contact with him to get his attention or make him move. Feeling those rock-hard biceps just about undid me. Being the recipient of his touches had been even worse.

Clearly, two months was far too long without some kind of physical release. Otherwise, how on earth could I be attracted to a guy like that? A guy whose career was in the toilet and who obviously had some serious unresolved family issues that I wanted to steer clear of. But apparently, my body didn't care which male the physical contact came from, so long as it arrived. From now on I'd keep my distance, far enough away that he couldn't stretch out his arm and get his fingertips anywhere near my lower back. Or any other part of me.

I sat up and bile rose up in my throat. I rocketed to the bathroom, grateful my hair was already tied back from when I'd been barfing last night. This vomiting thing was getting ridiculous. Maybe I'd see a doctor today.

Yeah, I'd squeeze that in between Sebastian's lunch with my dad, then the meeting with the record producer and, lastly, showing up at the restaurant grand opening for an acquaintance of his — the last two being perfectly good media opportunities I couldn't let Sebastian pass up.

I grabbed onto the edge of the sink and pulled myself up. Just as I reached for my toothbrush to de-grossify, my cell chimed. I darted back to my bedside to read Sebastian's text.

Couldn't do any songwriting last night. Wasn't feeling very creative. I was able to open the Facebook app tho and already have a few thousand followers. Don't know what I'm doing there and don't want to screw up live stream. Come and help?

He had so many followers because I'd set up his

profile and had been managing his posts — which were really my posts. I checked the time on my cell. Only eight o'clock, which gave us four hours before we had to meet with my dad for lunch. *See you in an hour*, I texted back.

I cruised up his street right on time, punched in the code to get through the gate, and sprinted to the front porch. I knocked three times before the door swung open.

Sebastian stood there in a pair of faded jeans, naked from the waist up and his skin damp. "Sorry, just got out of the shower. Hang on and I'll finish getting dressed."

As much as it pained me to say... "You're about to go live. Girls will be watching, lots of them. They'll stick around longer if they get to see this." I wagged a finger to encompass the length of him. Squeezing past him, I tried to unknow he was about to spend the next hour, at least, without a shirt. *Do not look at his happy trail.*

"Here." He tossed his phone at me and I glanced up just in time to catch it as I claimed a section of his sofa. "Crash course," he said, flopping down right next to me, his weight lowering the cushion and tilting me toward him. I gritted my teeth, determined to ignore the feel of his leg against mine.

"Let's try Periscope for live streaming, since you have more followers there, even though I only know enough to get by. I'm better on Twitter and Facebook." Pressing the button at the side, I woke up his phone. "First off, this doesn't require a password. If you lose it, anyone can access your entire life." I rolled my eyes at him, because believing he was an idiot kept the growing lust at bay. "All anyone has to do is turn it off and then you can't locate it. If this gets into the wrong hands, all our hard work could be undone. Add a password."

"Yes, ma'am." He grinned.

My irritation amused him? Whatever. I downloaded the Periscope app, then opened it and logged him in, then flashed him the screen. "From the little TV icon, you see the red button? Click it." I hit the button, then turned the screen toward him again. "Next, you type in the name of the broadcast. We'll go with something like... Full Throttle's Sebastian Trevino chilling at home."

He nodded. "Then what?"

"You click 'start broadcast' and talk. But just a couple things first, so you know how it works. Not that I'm an expert." I quickly searched for a current broadcast that might be even remotely interesting and then clicked on it. I readjusted the phone to make sure he could share the screen with me. "See how you tap it and you can send hearts? And right here, you can type stuff. See the comments popping up?"

"How am I going to read that crap while I'm in the middle of writing a song?"

I blew out a resigned breath. "I'll help you until you get the hang of it."

"Great." He hunted up a pad of paper and a couple pencils, then retrieved his guitar on the other side of the couch. "Let's do this."

I aimed the phone at Sebastian and hit the button, giving him a thumbs-up so he'd know he was live.

"I'm Sebastian Trevino. You might know me as the guitarist from Full Throttle." He squinted at the screen and laughed. "Thanks, I've been working out. A lot, actually." He shook his head. "No, not dating anyone. We're going on tour in a couple of months. My jeans?" He squinted. "I'm not into clothes at all, kinda old school. Usually just whatever seems good at the time." He looked closer at the questions popping up, then burst out laughing. "No, not taking them off for this broadcast. My workout routine? It's hard core right now. I do weights every other day, usually run four miles the other days. But I do a lot of other stuff in between, like planks, salmon ladder."

"I think we all want to see you on the salmon ladder," I said. No way was I going to pass that up. "Really, I think everyone needs to see that and get it out of the way so we can concentrate on what we're here for. Come on. I'll read the questions for you while your hands are busy. Where's your gym?"

His head swung side to side. "You guys don't want to see some guy on a salmon ladder, do you?" He stared at his phone and his shoulders drooped. "Seriously?"

Guessing all the comments were urging us to the gym, I flashed him a triumphant smile. I was confident that writing a song and creating a melody would have garnered a lot of viewers, but working out with *that* body? They'd stick around. And that's what we wanted — witnesses to him being involved in a clean activity.

With the camera aimed on his muscular backside, I trailed behind him as he led us to his gym at the other end of the huge house. I made the camera pan the room, showing the audience two treadmills standing in one corner. Next to it were various sets of weights and benches. I aimed the camera at the other side of the room where a wide ladder sat with rungs set about ten inches apart and a long pole resting horizontally on one of them. I was dying to watch Sebastian on that thing, working up a sweat.

"Hey, I just realized women love seeing men work poles." I snickered. "We just like them horizontal, while men want their women on a vertical pole."

"Very funny." He stood under the salmon ladder, glancing over at me and the camera.

"Tell us how it works," I said.

"The idea is to jump the pole to the next higher rung. You have to create a little momentum." He wrapped his hands at each end of the pole, pulled himself up and swung back and forth. His legs moved back again and forward, building momentum, and then he jumped the pole up the next notch. His stomach bunched and bulged, making my lips part, as he swung again and then moved up the next rung. He dropped to the ground.

"That's how it's done, folks," I said, still aiming his phone at him. My heart beat a little faster and my stomach fluttered. "But I think they need to see that again, Sebastian."

"You gotta be kidding me." He gave me the stink-eye and snatched the phone from me to look at the screen and read the comments. "Fine, one more time."

Struggling to keep a straight face and not drool, I trained the camera on him as he did it again. Up several rungs, then he lowered to the floor. "That's enough for one day."

I thrust the camera at him as he abandoned the salmon ladder. He leaned in to read the comments. "No, she's not my girlfriend. Does she want to be?" He chuckled. "I doubt it. Yeah, she's crazy. I agree."

"Not everyone falls madly in love with you, Sebastian," I said, taking on an irritated tone. "Some of us don't date musicians."

Grinning, he read the comments silently, shaking his head. Dying to read them myself and forgetting that our goal was keeping him in the spotlight, I flipped the phone around. The comments scrolled up and disappeared faster than I could catch some of them. But I got a few. "No, I'm not sleeping with him. Of course I don't plan to. Because I'm not interested." I propped the phone up against one of his clean towels on the shelf and spun around to find him over my shoulder grinning.

"They want to know who you are." He glanced at me with a lopsided smile, probably grateful the attention was off him for the moment. "Tell them."

"I'm just here helping him make some adjustments in his life." I stepped out of the shot and backed up.

Sebastian picked up the phone and aimed it at me. "Not so fast. They have more questions." He was barely suppressing his laughter.

"Then you answer them." My gaze fell to his ripped stomach and how it shined with a light layer of sweat from that delicious workout he'd just had. I sidestepped out of the camera's way.

"Ellie450 wants to know your name." He glanced at the screen again. "And how you know me."

I tried to grab the camera to get myself out of the frame, but he held it too high. Somehow he managed to keep it aimed on me. "Give it to me," I demanded, leaping up again in hopes of snagging the phone.

He brought it closer, but blocked me with his other hand when I reached for it. I could see my face on the screen and hearts floating along the side. Still, I wasn't convinced that I needed to be the center of anyone's attention. I sprung up again, reached for the phone, but he swung his arm back and I missed.

"I'm going to hurt you." My eyes went to the screen again as comments scrolled up faster than ever, a mass of hearts completely covering the side. This time, I jumped and grabbed with both hands, bumping into him. His naked chest pressed against my shoulder and a shiver began in my middle and spread out. I leaped back. "You're dead."

He snickered and adjusted the camera's view. "Isn't she pretty?" He eyed the screen as dozens of replies posted. "See? They agree."

Heat swept over my cheeks. "Only because you put them on the spot."

Sebastian shook his head as he scanned the comments more carefully. "No, you're wrong. The guys are the ones mostly commenting and if they didn't think you were hot, they'd just lay low."

While he wasn't watching me, I sprung again and snatched the phone. Twisting around, I moved forward to run, but Sebastian grabbed me by the waist and spun me around. With all my strength, I pushed off. He pulled me back but overcompensated and he lost his footing, sending us diving toward the ground. His back broke my fall, and I landed flush on top of him, my hip fitting perfectly against his.

God, he felt good, all firm and sexy. I froze. My lips parted and my gaze dropped to his mouth. His fingers wound through my hair and fisted, then he yanked me a tiny bit closer. Phone forgotten with no idea where it went, I pressed my palms against his chest and rolled off. Had I seriously almost kissed Sebastian? What was I thinking? Darting over to my right, I spied the phone and dived for it.

"And we're back, folks. Would you like more Q and A with Sebastian or do you want to see him play guitar?" I shot Sebastian a smug look.

"Game on," he whispered, skulking toward me.

My eyes stretched wide in horror, my palms flew up. "Hold on. I think they'd rather watch..." My gaze automatically drew to his gorgeous six-pack, "...what *you* have going on. I say we let the people vote."

His lip curled up. "Deal. Let's find out." He sidled up to me and we shared the phone, our eyes devouring the comments to learn the verdict.

More salmon ladder... We want to see you both get sweaty... You two need to release some sexual frustration... That was some serious foreplay... Give her that kiss you both want... Less clothes... Lose the jeans... Whatever you did while we couldn't see, do it again for us.

Oh, crap. "Sorry, folks, nothing happened. We just lost our balance and fell."

"I got a nice handful of her ass, though." He wiggled his brows. "Firm."

I blinked, pivoted on my heel, then bolted and grabbed my purse on the way to the front door. Without even a goodbye, I flew outside, took the two steps at record speed and scrambled into my car. Making out with Sebastian was already a temptation without someone else voting me into it. I would never Periscope with him again. He and his perverted fans were on their own.

I started the engine of the Lexus and hurried through the gate as soon as it opened for me. When my car hit asphalt, I peeled away with my heart thumping.

A part of me wished I could stay and give in to the lust. I wanted to feel those lips against mine, but this time I wanted him sober and aware of every part of me that he touched. And every part of him I touched. A shiver teased my stomach and I pushed away the fantasy. Not going to happen. Musicians and actors were too self-centered and thought they were better than everyone else. Most of them didn't even have a proper education and I didn't want a partner who couldn't keep up with me. I wouldn't mind outthinking my partner once in a while, but not all the time.

I steered my car farther from his house, down the lush, tree-lined street and wondered if he had returned to his broadcast or signed out. With curiosity killing me, I pulled over, signed into my Periscope account and located his broadcast. His profile popped up on my screen and my stomach dipped.

Sebastian's guitar neck lay on his thigh as he leaned over to scribble on a pad. Since he wasn't looking at his screen, he didn't see me join the broadcast. My lungs deflated in relief.

"You need a theme first. Otherwise, the song has no direction, no message. I suppose you could have a song with a bunch of words that don't really mean anything. Some people get away with that. I prefer a little more substance myself." He tapped the pencil's eraser against his chin, then leaned toward his phone and eyed the comments. "My inspiration? Whatever makes me feel passionate at the moment, I guess. Songs can go all sorts of ways. It can tell a whole story, or deal with a specific problem or it can include a happy ending."

Write something about the hot redhead...

Bad idea! But if I typed my thoughts in the comments, Sebastian would know I was watching. I gripped the phone in my hands, my knees clenched together, praying he didn't write anything about me.

Sebastian's brows lifted, an amused smile sneaking across his face. "That's an idea. I think she's worthy of her own song. Now, I can't just say this girl is hot and that we're not right for each other. We need more than that, so I have to pump it up, you know? Exaggerate it a bit." Sebastian's eyes darted to the screen for an instant before returning to his note pad. "Maybe something like... She's testing my will... but I'll resist until..." Sebastian studied the ceiling a moment, then jotted something on the pad. His fingers stilled, then he furiously scribbled out a bunch of the words, then began writing again. "She crosses that line, and I'll make her mine."

The screen flooded with hearts. I tossed my phone aside in disgust, not knowing if I could bear to hear him write an entire song about me. I doubted it would be favorable. Besides, I couldn't sit on the side of the road forever. I needed to pee.

Putting my car into gear, my gaze drifted to my phone. Sebastian's face smiled up at me and I reached over to turn up the volume.

"She's liquid fire, brings on the hurt. She's Satan's hire in a mini skirt."

Oh, he had to be kidding. My knuckles whitened as I negotiated a turn. I was going to murder him — in about an hour or so when he came over to meet with my dad for lunch.

"I'm giving up, and I've given in. C'mon, girl, don't leave me hangin'," a voice sang from my phone.

That didn't even rhyme properly. Well, maybe, depending on how it was sung. Wait... he was writing that song loosely based on me. Did that mean I was his inspiration for the words? Was he actually attracted to me?

I might've resented him a little less if not for the fact that he'd already had his curiosity satisfied with me. He'd already been there, done that with me, yet my attraction to him hadn't waned at all. If anything, it had become increasingly more intense. Maybe if he hadn't been working out so hard these past two months, I may have been spared. But, no, he looked amazing.

My car rolled down the long driveway of my dad's house and I parked it in front of the guest house. Once I'd made it into my little house, I slipped off my boots and then practically fell onto my couch. I didn't even have the energy to find the remote, just stared at the blank screen on the TV.

★

Sandpaper scraped my eyes as I strained to lift my lids. Was someone knocking? I heard pounding again and leaped up to get the door, practically tripping over my shoes. My dad would've let himself in after a quick tap, which meant the knocker was someone else. But who? I rarely got visitors. I'd spent too much time in school and college taking extra classes, or enrolled in accelerated programs, to form any lasting bonds.

Still foggy in the head, I swung the door open. I automatically touched what must have been very messy hair, and stared into deep brown eyes. "What are you doing here?"

Sebastian rocked back on his heels. "I was going to ask you the same thing." When I gave him a blank look, he pointed at his wrist. Except he wasn't wearing a watch. "You're late."

I scrunched my nose up. "Crap. I fell asleep. I need to make sure I'm not scary. I'll just be a minute. Maybe you should come in and make sure I actually make it the twenty yards into the house." Sadly, I was serious. Without him right there, I would have probably returned to the couch and fallen asleep. I rolled my eyes at my own patheticness, turned, and left the door open for him to follow.

In my peripheral vision, Sebastian crossed the threshold, his eyes taking in the worn brown leather couch, the scuffed chest I used as a coffee table, and the antique dining room table made from a pine slab that had been left unfinished except for the dark staining. He slowed, his eyes becoming fixed on the brass spittoon on the wash table. "So not what I expected your place to look like."

"What did you expect?" I glugged some water as I waited for his reply, taking that time to slough off the sleep.

Sebastian lifted a shoulder, his gaze lowering to the wide plank hardwood floors. "A lot of white, more modern..."

I scoffed, anger brewing in my chest. "You mean sterile and cold?"

"Uhm." He shook his head. "No, just clean and light."

"You suck at lying. This is the one place I can truly relax. I want it warm and friendly." My stomach rumbled. "What's for lunch, do you know?"

"Fish, I think." He shrugged.

"Fish?" My stomach churned and I grimaced. "Sounds disgusting."

Sebastian dipped his head to the side, narrowing his eyes. "Your dad said it was one of your favorites."

"Was. *Was* my favorite. Not today." I pressed my lips together, hoping I wouldn't have to run to the bathroom. I was supposed to be getting ready and I was already late. I didn't need to be delayed by a vomiting session.

Sebastian leaned forward and whispered, "Are you pregnant?"

I froze, my gaze riveting to his. "What?"

"I was around while Liam's sister Faith was pregnant. She slept at random times, couldn't hold much food down, and her appetite changed. And she was very cranky." He shrugged, but he didn't take his eyes of me. "Kind of like you."

"I can't be pregnant. Impossible." Wasn't it? I kept track of my period religiously and I hadn't missed one. Since it had already been over two months since I'd been with Sebastian, I couldn't possibly be knocked up. I shook my head. "No, definitely not. No way."

"So you haven't been with anyone?" He blinked and waved a hand. "Sorry, none of my business. Just wondering how you can be so sure."

My mouth dropped open. Idiot! I'd been with *him*. I closed my mouth, trying to come up with a reply that wouldn't blast him.

"Hey, I'm not trying to be nosy. If you weren't with anyone, then you weren't. I believe you. Like I said, none of my business. But if you can't be pregnant, then maybe it's something else and you should see a doctor."

Oh. My. God. Sebastian didn't remember our night of wild sex. My face hurt from the effort to hold back the outrage consuming me.

But how could I stay mad at him for ignoring something that he wasn't even aware of? I'd been taking him far too seriously. I pulled air into my lungs, then released it and let my shoulders relax.

My relief was replaced by regret. I'd been punishing him and he had no clue why. Granted, getting drunk and having sex with me was *his* doing. But I'd been there too and had equal responsibility. And if I wanted a guy to remember me, I needed to make sure he wasn't beyond wasted.

"If you really don't want to see a doctor yet, you can research your symptoms on line." His mouth twisted. "Never mind. Every time I do that, I always end up convinced I'm dying."

"If it doesn't let up soon, I'll see a doctor. I promise." I ducked into the bathroom. My hair was a little messy, but impressing Sebastian was the last thing I should care about. After slipping into my boots, I returned to Sebastian who was leafing through the notepad I'd left on the coffee table. "Let's go."

Struggling through the smell of fish, I followed Sebastian into the main house. My dad was putting the final touches on what any normal person would consider gourmet — halibut steak marinated in garlic and rosemary, rice pilaf and asparagus spears. Potato soup already steamed from a small bowl in front of each place setting. My dad didn't cook much, but when he did, it was usually pretty good.

Still, fish was a big no for me today, so I stuck to rice and vegetables. Once I'd dived in, I barely heard my dad and Sebastian talking business and only responded when they made it a point to get my feedback.

So Sebastian had a huge blank spot that night. Not only did he not remember the first round on his kitchen table before we'd gotten all my clothes off, he also didn't remember ravaging me again in his bed after a few shots of tequila.

I speared the last asparagus, feeling full. It had been weeks since I'd had an appetite and even then, I hadn't always kept it down. I hoped for the chance to fully digest all of it this time.

Sebastian's question nagged at me. I couldn't be pregnant, no way. I was a stickler for documenting my cycle and if I had missed a month, I would've realized it.

I glanced up at Sebastian who was enjoying another piece of halibut. He was way off about me possibly being pregnant, of course.

But what if he wasn't?

Proving him wrong suddenly became my life's mission. Not wanting to raise any red flags, I slowly pushed the chair away, dabbed the corners of my mouth with the cloth napkin and stood. "That was amazing, Dad, thank you. But I think I left the stove on earlier. I'd started to make tea and then fell asleep. I'll be back in a minute and help clean up."

My dad nodded while Sebastian shot me a

puzzled look. I shuffled out the back door as casually as I could. When I knew they couldn't hear or see me, I rocketed to the guest house and yanked my trusty calendar off the hook near my desk. I flipped to the previous month, October, examining each square. Nothing. Between arranging interviews for Full Throttle and working for my dad, as well as the other freelance public relations here and there, I must have forgotten to write it in. But I'd never once in ten years forgotten to mark it down.

There was a first time for everything though, right?

Unless I hadn't gotten my period at all.

I stared at the calendar another moment, then snatched up my purse and bolted out the door. Sebastian and my dad would wonder where I went and I didn't care. I had to do this, had to know.

Ten minutes later, I returned with two pregnancy tests. Very convenient since I really had to pee.

I'd had to pee a lot lately. And I was tired, napping at random times. My stomach had been more particular than ever and I'd never thrown up so much in such a short time in my whole life. And my breasts were painfully tender.

And there was no mark on the calendar for last month.

Oh, crap. I groaned, burying my eyes in my palms. *Please, no. Please don't let me be pregnant.*

I fervently hoped it was some odd hormone issue that would be easily rectified with black cohosh or maca powder.

After unwrapping the tester, I scanned the directions, then painstakingly followed them. I tapped my fingers as I waited the required minutes, my gaze glued to the clock on my phone. Finally, the time was up and I stared at the double blue lines.

My life was ruined.

In my heart of hearts, I had known before I got the results. Sebastian and I had made a real, live baby and it was growing inside me. It would gradually turn into an actual person and come into the world in about seven months.

And the father of the baby had no idea we'd even had sex.

With my elbows on the bathroom sink, I dropped my face into my palms. My stomach churned and I hoped I wasn't going to throw up.

Getting rid of the baby wasn't an option. I never judged other women for their decisions. Their bodies were just that — theirs. And the decision to have a baby was theirs and theirs alone. Everyone had their own beliefs and no matter how much anyone else disagreed with that belief, they had to suck it up. Because everyone had a right to think and feel however they chose. But I could never choose to consciously stop my own baby from existing. As much as I didn't want a baby right at this exact moment, I definitely wanted children someday.

Well, guess what, Violet, someday is now.

I'd gotten my master's degree three months ago and my career had just begun to roll. I was barely making enough money for food, gas and insurance for my car. How was I going to get through the next seven months, then deal with a newborn and still nurture my career? I was totally screwed and my eight-year plan just went *kaboom*!

CHAPTER SEVEN
★ *Sebastian* ★

By the time Violet sauntered back into the main house, her dad and I were just wrapping up the meeting. Her pale face matched the white of the walls, but her eyes resembled the Italian flag — red, white and green. I assumed she'd been worshipping the throne in her bathroom, which made me even more suspicious she was pregnant.

Maybe she was right and she had a virus. Guilt consumed me for making her work so hard on my reputation when she really should be resting. She should be in bed.

With me.

I shook off those thoughts. I was a glutton for punishment to consider sleeping with her when she had made her feelings about me extremely clear. She wasn't interested. I shouldn't have been interested either.

"Hey, sweetheart." Aidan beamed at her. "Feeling

okay?"

"Been better, but I'll survive. Sorry I missed most of the meeting." She sat on the coffee table in front of Aidan, giving me her profile. "Anything I need to know?"

"TMZ picked up footage of Sebastian's broadcast this morning," Aidan said. "As of a few minutes ago, he had already gotten over five thousand replay views. I've had several calls this morning wanting interviews, but they're smalltime. I told them to contact you."

"Good. It's already working," she said, still not looking at me. "And it's not even one thirty yet. Who knows what will happen next?" She held up her palm for a high five from her dad.

"I talked to Emerson today and he's got some plans for Sebastian," Aidan said. "He wasn't too cooperative a month ago, said he wanted to see how things went with Sebastian before they invested in PR. But he seems to be warming up now."

"Thanks, Dad. I appreciate you getting the ball rolling on so much of this. We're still on for three today with Emerson?"

"His secretary hasn't called to cancel."

"Good. We'll see him shortly and see for ourselves his attitude toward Sebastian." She ran a hand through her thick hair, exposing a handful of freckles on her shoulder.

My tongue yearned to play connect-the-dots on her skin.

"I was planning on lining up some musical gigs, like solo acts." Violet shifted so I couldn't see her face anymore. "Maybe have him sing backup on another track. He has a strong and unique voice."

"Or he can play guitar, maybe start with Outlaw Dogs." Aidan scratched his chin. "They're doing a lot of special appearances right now. They'd probably love to have him tag along on one of their spots."

"Good idea. I'll see if I can hook him up with some female singers who'd like him featured on their album." Violet tapped that full bottom lip. "I'll make a list and maybe you can get in touch with some of them."

What about me? Didn't they want my input? I huffed, leaning toward them so I could see their faces. "I'm sitting right here."

Violet twisted around, looked me square in the eye and lifted one brow. "No one's stopping you from pitching in. Wouldn't hurt you to share in the load, actually. It's your mess, after all."

"I guess my reprieve is over. Should've known the last twenty-four hours of you being nice were too good to be true." I tunneled my hand through my hair, shaking my head, then rose from the sofa. "I guess you guys can wrap up the meeting without me."

As I turned to go, Violet's voice had my legs rooted to the floor. "See you at the studio in forty-five minutes," she said.

With my back to them both, I raised a hand and wiggled my fingers, then I let myself out through the front door. I'd thought Violet had chilled a bit, but apparently not. I'd thought we had a moment in my gym earlier when she'd fallen on top of me. Wrong again.

But she'd never been a prospect anyway. I'd known how she was before she'd taken me on as a client. No surprises there. She'd had a kind and generous moment at the hospital yesterday, her saving grace. Other than that, and her amazing ass, she had no redeeming qualities. For her sake, I hoped she eased up or she wouldn't have any clients. Or she'd better be a miracle worker. Either way, I'd have to put up with her for the next few weeks. And, who knew? Maybe she'd get the job done faster and I could fire her ahead of schedule.

I cruised into the parking lot of the Burbank Mall, ready to walk the two blocks to the record label's office. I strolled toward Coffee Bean for some caffeine, my head bent down so I wouldn't be recognized — yeah, I needed exposure, but after being around Violet, getting a breather was a bigger priority. As I neared the entrance door a few yards ahead, a voice stopped me.

"You broke the ice, became my friend. I broke

free, was on the mend. Then you broke it off, despite my plea. You broke my heart, you broke me."

I zeroed in on the skinny black kid wailing away and strumming a custom Gibson in two-tone green. His guitar case lay open in front of his feet, crumpled bills lining the bottom. I hoped he made a good living. My head swaying to the music, I waited through the last note. "Nice runs, man. You have a great voice."

His mouth dropped open and he blinked. "Thank you, Mr. Trevino."

"If you get to keep all the money, would you mind if I backed you up?" I jerked my head toward the guitar. I could make time for one song. Besides, it had been too long since I'd performed in public just for the sheer joy of it.

The boy swallowed, then nodded briskly as he held out his Gibson. "Hell, yeah. You wanna do a Full Throttle song or something else?"

Hands tingling and my pulse racing, I reached for the guitar and tossed the strap over my head. "Liam's songs are working for you. How about *Blood is Gonna Spill*?"

He wiped his sweaty hands on the thighs of his jeans and took a deep breath. His toes began tapping and I counted along. I hit the first chord and the boy smiled, his head rocking with every strike of the string. "Again you hurt what's mine.

Again you crossed the line. Say you didn't break the law. And that's your fatal flaw."

Damn, this kid was good. I could feel my face splitting into a grin. The boy beamed at me and went into the chorus. "You won't get another chance to put me in a trance. This time I won't stand still. Your blood is gonna spill. Will overflow onto the road, until you've paid what's owed."

I hitched up a thumb when he ripped into the next verse and he visibly relaxed, pacing in front of the crowd that had formed around us. His body moved to the music and he made more eye contact with the audience. I grinned as arms shot out from the crowd and people leaned toward the guitar case to fill it with money.

He drew out the last note and the crowd cheered and clapped. I returned the guitar to the boy, then held out my hand. "What's your name?"

He gave my hand a brisk shake, then let it go. "Diego."

"Good to meet you. I have to go, but thanks for letting me sit in. Best of luck to you." I nodded, but Diego just stood there dumbstruck. I would've loved to do another song with him, but then I'd be late for the meeting with Emerson. The record label executives already thought I was a jackass. They didn't need that opinion fueled by me being late and wasting their time. I was already on thin ice with Violet, and didn't want her any harder to deal with.

Skipping my coffee stop since I'd already used up any extra time, I continued to the meeting. And Violet. Though it had been less than an hour since I'd left her dad's place, my stomach tightened at the thought of seeing her again. I tried to convince myself that my reaction to her was purely a side effect from my stress level going up due to her crazy mood swings. That lie lasted about a second.

How I would've loved to finish what we'd started in the gym of my house, just turn off the damn phone and run my hands up her side, maybe get a bigger handful of her ass as she pressed against me. I shook my head to clear out those thoughts. Man, if I could be that attracted to a girl like Violet, I really needed to get laid.

Inside the building, the elevator door dinged, then swished open and I dashed inside. It climbed and dinged again before stopping. As soon as I stepped out and into the reception area toward the wide, circular counter, Aidan and Violet each rose from their chair and met me halfway. Aidan clapped me on the shoulder, then whispered, "Remember what we talked about at lunch, the three Ds for success: decision, direction, discipline. Decide what you want to do, set your goal, then stick to it. Show them you can do it."

That didn't seem like any fun at all. Not that I required a nonstop party and I was perfectly capable of focusing when necessary. I didn't mind working long hours or sacrificing sleep for something I loved. But passion had led me to music. The three Ds sucked all the passion out of anything. I would play along anyway and do my best to make Aidan and the execs happy. Not like I had a choice.

My gaze landed on Violet, who was riveted to her phone screen. Aidan followed my line of sight. "What's the status, sweetheart?" he asked.

Her eyes bugged out. "It hit TMZ and YouTube, already has over seven thousand views. Facebook has close to three hundred shares. Unbelievable."

"What are you guys talking about?" I asked, trying to get a glimpse of the screen.

"In less than ten minutes?" Aidan asked as if I were invisible, eyeing her phone more closely.

"People perceive it as something with heart, something they didn't expect at all. Actually, some people are saying it was staged. But we know it wasn't." Violet squinted her eyes and touched the screen with a fingertip. "Just refreshed. Another fifty shares on Facebook."

I opened my mouth to interrogate them when the president of Vista Records approached, his arms wide in welcome and a bright smile on his face — which I would've appreciated if I thought

Emerson was sincere. Not that he was a complete douche, but ultimately money was his only god.

"Sebastian, good to see you." He clasped my hand an instant before taking Violet's and bending to drop a kiss on the back of it. He straightened again, refocusing on Aidan. "Let's step into my office."

"You look radiant," Emerson told Violet as he ushered us into his lavish office. He offered us seats and then took the chair behind the gleaming walnut desk. "Never seen you look more beautiful."

"Thank you." She offered him a warm smile. "How are Charlotte and Nathan?"

Why didn't she share those sweet smiles with me? She'd been nice to the wait staff when we'd gone out to eat, she'd been kind to my fans, and she'd even treated the hospital staff with respect. Except for that brief period when I was looking for my mom and a few moments while we were on Periscope, she'd treated me like vermin. What the hell did I do wrong?

"Charlotte's graduating high school and Nathan just got his braces off."

"That's wonderful." She flashed him another smile. "Give them a hug for me."

"So...," Aidan began, relaxing into the chair next to me. "Looks like we're on track for the concert tour. Sebastian should be appearing totally cleaned up in the next few weeks. Violet, would you like to fill him in on our most recent victory?"

"Fill me in on what?" Emerson asked, his brows pinched in skepticism.

"See for yourself." She abandoned her chair to stand beside Emerson. After tapping her phone a few times, she aimed the screen at him. An extremely poor-quality recording of *Blood is Gonna Spill* streamed from her phone. I'd just heard that a few minutes ago down the street. That was Diego's voice. "Wait until the end," she told Emerson.

I heard myself thanking Diego for letting me sit in and wishing him luck. Okay, so someone had recorded it, but I didn't get why Violet was showing it to Emerson.

"Already hit TMZ and has thousands of YouTube views. Fans are thinking he's a god." Aidan sat straighter in his chair, a proud look on his face. "A little more coverage like this and you won't have to worry about record sales due to the band's reputation."

"Are you kidding me?" Emerson laughed once. "Record sales are based on bad reps and notoriety. I'm just worried about getting sued."

"Guys, I'm right here." My mouth skewed in disgust. "You're not going to get sued, Emerson. I'm not drinking or partying anymore. Honestly, I kind of lost my taste for it."

Emerson slapped his palms down and pushed off his desk to loom over us. "I'm glad to hear it. If everything goes as planned, you'll be on tour in a few months. Thanks for coming by." He did the rounds, shaking our hands, then showed us to the door.

Once in the elevator, Violet rounded on me. "If you could refrain from public performances without my approval, I would appreciate it. You got lucky that this one worked in your favor, but next time, you might not be so fortunate."

"I'm a grown man, Violet. I'm capable of mature activities without adult supervision."

She gritted her teeth, then whirled around to face the front of the elevator. As soon as the door opened, she bolted like she couldn't get away from me fast enough, and threw over her shoulder, "I'll be at your house in two hours, Sebastian. Please try not to make any waves until then. I'll meet you at the car, Dad."

As she raced ahead, leaving us in her dust, Aidan's head whipped around to me, his brows way up and his eyes wide. "What the hell did you do to piss her off?"

I shrugged. "I was wondering the same thing. I've been hoping it was just my imagination."

He chuckled, shaking his head. "Unfortunately, it's very real. I've never seen her like that." He slapped me on the shoulder. "Good luck at the opening."

Yeah, I was going to need it. "See you." I backtracked into the building and exited out the front, remembering I'd parked two blocks away. At the curb, I stopped for the red light before crossing.

I'd always been nice to Violet, but that didn't matter to her. She was determined to dislike me, regardless what I did. Well, I was finished trying to appease her. If she was going to be mad at me anyway, what was the point in going out of my way for her? If how I acted meant nothing, then I could say or do whatever I wanted. I'd see if she could take the rudeness as well as she dished it out.

Or maybe I'd be charming. That would mess with her head and make things interesting. Either scenario, I itched to see her reaction.

For the first time since beginning this new image-shaping, I was looking forward to my next publicity task — and seeing Violet.

CHAPTER EIGHT
★ *Violet* ★

I headed to Sebastian's house, wishing I had scheduled his appearances and our meetings further apart, rather than so many in one day. After starting early that day on Periscope with him, lunch at my dad's house and then a meeting with Emerson, I was fried. But I still had to get through the restaurant grand opening. My fuzzy brain wanted sleep and my foot strained with the effort to push on the accelerator. I hoped they started on time and that Sebastian didn't want to stay late. The baby and I needed our beauty rest.

The baby... I was pregnant with Sebastian's child and he had no clue. Because he'd been careless and gotten too drunk to remember the act, much less me. And because I'd been naive, and had allowed myself to get caught up in the moment with the hot rock star, I had no one to blame but myself. My life would never be the same.

How the hell was I going to juggle a career and be a single mom? Since Full Throttle had won a Grammy and had become so successful, money was flooding into my dad's bank account. He had paid off his pretty little house and no longer had to worry financially. Very likely, he would help me with the baby. But mooching off him wasn't an option for me. I was living in his guest house, but I paid rent. Usually.

Between the nausea, the fatigue and the terror of raising a child alone when I couldn't yet fully support myself, I was so tied up in knots, I couldn't think straight. Being nice to the guy who helped get me there, and who was too clueless to realize it, was a low priority.

By the time I pulled up in front of his house, I had worked myself into a frenzy. I threw my head against the driver's seat and hissed. What was I going to do about Sebastian? I had to tell him about his baby, obviously, but I couldn't bring myself to do it. Not just yet.

Very soon Sebastian's life and career would be on track again and we'd see very little of each other. I had no idea if he was even interested in playing daddy. If I carried the baby to term, I'd have to tell him before it was born. Ideally, long before then.

I'd figure it out soon. For now, I was comforted by the knowledge that my rollercoaster emotions and wild lust for him stemmed from my out of control pregnancy hormones. None of those feelings were due to me actually liking Sebastian.

Other than the baby, Sebastian and I had nothing in common, no connection whatsoever. And a baby did not a relationship make. I had to get over my resentment toward him, purge the anger from my head, and do my best to create a relationship with him as a co-parent.

I'd be decent to him. But I didn't have to like him.

Reluctant to get out of my car, I texted him to let him know I had arrived and to come outside. I wouldn't offer up any nasty comments, no glares. I was determined to behave. He didn't need to be as miserable as I was.

I sucked in a long, slow breath, then released it. Without the fan on, the air in my car had become stagnant and I rolled down the window as Sebastian's head appeared through the opening, his fingers gripping the door.

"Hey, gorgeous." He flashed me that same smile that had lured me into his bedroom.

I tingled all over as I looked at him all freshly showered and smelling of mint. Annoyed with myself, I scowled at him, wondering what he was up to. "Get in."

"Sure you don't want me to drive?"

Lately, driving had been trying because I didn't

feel as alert as usual. The less time I spent behind the wheel, the better. Especially when all I wanted to do was crawl into bed and sleep for a week. "Knock yourself out."

He stepped away as I opened the car door and climbed out. I moved to go around him but he blocked me, his arms caging me in against my car. "So... I was mulling over your hostility toward me."

I shot him a scathing look. As much as I wanted to be nice, I couldn't do that if he pushed me. "Are we sharing our feelings now?"

A smug smile spread over his face. "Not *my* feelings. Yours. Must be some powerful emotions to make you dislike me so much."

I rolled my eyes. "That makes no sense."

"Exactly." He leaned in to whisper in my ear. "What you're feeling toward me isn't dislike at all, is it?"

Was this asshat hinting that I had a thing for him? Oh, he had no idea! I shoved the ball of my hand into his chest. "It's just good old-fashioned disgust." I stormed to the passenger's side, determined to ignore him. So much for trying to build a relationship.

"Mm-hmm." He slipped behind the wheel. "Whatever you say."

He smirked as he backed us out of the driveway. I don't know what pissed me off more, his assuming

I had feelings for him or that he had figured out that there was more to my feelings than I had let on.

Somehow, I was even more drawn to him now. That said, my libido would probably act up around any hot guy I was exposed to. Grinding my teeth, I forced myself not to utter another word to him. I stayed faithful to that vow the entire trip.

Thankfully, Sebastian went for valet parking again and I didn't have to walk several blocks in high heeled boots to get to Sunset Boulevard. Climbing out of my car, I smoothed down my short skirt. Sebastian appeared in front of me, offering his hand. I ignored it and he snickered. Jerk. Once we arrived at the entrance to the restaurant, I steeled myself to stay focused and concentrate on my job.

Once inside the restaurant, I kept my distance and let Sebastian do his thing. Eventually, I found a spot in the corner and whipped out my phone to catch up on my emails, still observing Sebastian on the sly. In between sampling from the delicious array of appetizers the restaurant had set out, while not touching any offered drinks, he charmed everyone. That earned him my reluctant admiration for his ability to schmooze.

Finished with all the work I could do from my phone, I rubbed my eyes and yawned, wishing the night would just end already. And it was only six-thirty. From my spot out of the way, I located

Sebastian who was flashing his sexy grin at a busty blonde. Of course he was. I'd been so busy seeing him as a loser who'd messed up his life that I'd never noticed the degree of charisma he possessed. He was a gorgeous specimen of a man and, as much as I didn't want to admit it, he was sweet and sincere. And he was a celebrity. Any girl would be lucky to snag him.

And they knew it. The blonde certainly did. I could tell by the way she brushed her arm against his and how her thumb dug into his bicep. A spike of jealousy slapped me and I blinked.

I really needed to stop ogling him.

His gaze cut to mine before I had a chance to avert my own. His eyes narrowed for a minute, then he returned to the blonde and lowered his lips to her cheek, pausing at her ear for what were probably sweet nothings. Abruptly, he backed away from her, then strode in my direction.

"We should head out. I have some lyrics burning a hole in my brain. You ready?" He rocked his head toward the exit.

Yep, more than ready. "Sure. But what's the rush?"

"Like I said, lyrics. Gotta get them down before I forget them."

"You don't bring a note pad with you? Even better, you could install a recording app on your phone."

"I haven't gotten around to it. Besides, not much opportunity to leave the house the last few weeks, so I've always had paper handy."

Right, because he'd been in rehab or home.

We spent the next few minutes trying to escape, but kept getting derailed. Everyone wanted a piece of Sebastian. At least I wasn't the only one. Finally, we stepped out into the cool air and I shivered.

Sebastian handed the ticket to the valet, then studied me a moment. "You cold?"

I rolled my eyes. "I'm cold. I'm hot. It's hard to keep up. But right now, yeah, I'm freezing." My teeth chattered on the last word and I hugged myself.

He took off his leather jacket and wrapped it around my shoulders.

"Thank you." The scent of him blanketed me, making me want to snuggle against him and burrow my face into his neck. I inhaled a little more, then I groaned inwardly at my unwanted desire to be around Sebastian. I doubted I'd be this drawn to him if my test had come back negative. This pregnancy, and all the emotions that went with it, was ruining my life. Seven more months of this onslaught of extreme hormones? Ugh.

Getting off Sunset Boulevard took forever and by the time we arrived at his house, I'd already nodded off three times. As he navigated my car into his driveway so I could drop him off, I rubbed my eyes in an effort to wake up enough to get myself home.

Sebastian climbed out of my car, but not before he killed the engine and pocketed the keys. I scurried around to the other side just in time to reach him before he disappeared inside. "Hey, you forgot something." I held out my hand, palm up.

"Come inside a minute," he threw over his shoulder as he unlocked the door.

"This isn't a date and I'm tired. I'm going home." I stayed outside, waiting for him to come back.

"Not without your car key," he called out from inside.

Damn him. What game was he playing? I had no choice but to find out. "Sebastian, I need to go. For the love of God, please give me my keys."

"I want to show you something."

Groaning, I followed his voice through his house and around the corner, spotting him at the end of the hallway. He hitched a thumb toward an open door. "Check it out."

I peeked into the spacious room. A black and gray pattern rug partially covered beautiful hardwood floors. The thick, black spread over the queen-size sleigh bed looked soft and inviting. I took a step back and created a distance between Sebastian and I. "Why are you showing me your bedroom?"

He laughed. "It's not my bedroom. It's yours. For a little while anyway. As long as it takes for you to be rested enough to drive." I opened my mouth to deny being incapable or helpless, but he forged on, grasping my shoulders. "Violet, you're exhausted. And if you leave like this, fall asleep at the wheel or something, I'll never forgive myself."

I could be stubborn, but the truth was that I dreaded the thought of driving. Sebastian was right. I was beyond beat. "Okay. But please don't let me sleep longer than like a half hour. I still have a lot to do tonight."

"Sleep at least a half hour and I'll give you back your keys. As soon as you're alert enough to drive." He held up his hand as though he were making an official pledge.

"Fine." I brushed past him, already eager to get on that bed. My fingers clasped the lapels of his jacket and I slipped it off and handed it to him. "Thanks for this."

He took the leather from me and turned to go, then stopped abruptly and spun back around. "Does Aidan know?"

I sat on the bed and kicked off my shoes. "Know about what?"

He raised one brow. "The baby."

Yeah, okay, so I wasn't fooling Sebastian. But knowing the truth was probably better than him thinking I had some horrible disease. And if anyone had a right to know I was pregnant, it was him. I just wasn't ready yet to tell him the baby was his. "Nobody else knows. I just found out earlier today, actually."

He nodded, absorbing that information.

"Why were you so sure?" I wrinkled my nose. "It could've been a stomach bug, like I thought."

"I would've bought that line you were feeding me. Actually, I totally did — until I noticed today how often you touch your stomach." His gaze dropped.

I followed his line of vision. Yep, there was my palm, flattened against my tummy. My hand whipped away and I made a mental note to be more careful in the future. "If you could keep this quiet, I'd appreciate it. I'm not ready to tell my dad that his daughter just threw away her entire future because of one crazy night."

His head rocked forward in response. "No problem. But you didn't throw away your future, Violet. You still have one. There's just a kid in it now."

He had a point. Still... "You're going to act like an unplanned pregnancy wouldn't throw you off at all?"

"If I found out someone out there was pregnant with my child..." He shrugged. "I've always imagined myself with kids one day, but in that vision, I'm married. If it happened another way, yes, I'd be surprised. And then I'd figure out how to work with the mom."

So he was actually okay with kids? I swallowed, knowing I'd never be able to get out of telling him. And I would tell him. But not today. I brought one knee up on the bed and rested an elbow on it. "Yeah, I know you're right. But nothing will ever be the same and..." I'd been about to say that I was scared.

"It's going to be okay, Violet. Aidan's going to be thrilled when you tell him."

I swallowed back tears, not wanting Sebastian to see me lose it. I couldn't meet Sebastian's gaze, just focused on the curtain billowing at the window. "Yeah, I wasn't worried about that."

He leaned against the doorframe. "You're worried about the guy's reaction when you tell him he's going to be a daddy?"

"You know some guys. They offer all kinds of things out of duty. I'd never know if his feelings were real or if he was only doing the right thing."

"The guy's a moron if he doesn't appreciate you." Sebastian's spine straightened. "If he doesn't do right by you, let me know and I'll have a word with him."

I chuckled. "I'll handle it, but thanks."

The toe of his boot kicked at something I couldn't see. "Want some water or something?"

I smiled. Sebastian could be sweet when he wanted to be, defending me against a guy he thought might hurt me, offering me a place to sleep.

Something told me his little display of douchiness earlier had been an act. It was the only time I'd seen him behave like an ape.

"I'm good. But thanks." He had the door half way closed when my voice stopped him. "Sebastian?"

He popped his head through the doorway. "Yeah?"

"Thanks for the place to crash."

He lifted his chin in acknowledgment and the door clicked shut. I collapsed against the pillow, closed my eyes and I was out.

★

Lifting my lids was like trying to slide Velcro sideways. Extremely difficult. After I finally triumphed over the desire to keep sleeping, I rolled off the bed. I made a quick stop in the bathroom to check my hair in the mirror — and pee, of course — then slogged into the living room. Sebastian sat on the floor, leaning against the front of the couch, the side of a guitar resting on his thighs. He didn't glance my way as he turned the little knobs to tighten the strings, a pad riddled with scribbles lying in front of him on the floor.

I slunk into the shadows, not wanting him to see me watching him. I wanted to hear him sing, watch him work magic with words.

"Tell me the dark won't last forever. Baby, tell me

things'll get better. I want to live, just don't know how. Not even you can save me now." Sebastian tested out some chords, then tried out another. Then he went back to the original chord as he sang the chorus. "I'll be free from you at last, no longer haunted by the past."

Thankfully, this time that I'd walked in on him writing lyrics, he was wearing a shirt. Granted, it was a tank top and his bulky biceps were saying hello in the most distracting way possible, but at least I wouldn't be assaulted by that six-pack. Damn, he was hot.

"Are you going to join me or stand there all night?" he asked, leaning over to jot something down on the pad.

"When I interrupted you yesterday, you stopped playing. I didn't want to disturb you again." Heat warmed my cheeks and I was glad he hadn't looked at me. His lack of eye contact obviously meant he wasn't interested in me. Didn't matter how much I lusted after his body, there was no real connection between us. I knew it. He knew it. "Those lyrics are pretty dark."

"Wrote them after my sister disappeared." His fingertips skated across the guitar strings. "So you haven't told the father?"

"Back to the baby, are we?" I grimaced. "I'm about nine weeks pregnant. Risk of miscarriage decreases dramatically after the first trimester. Figured I'd wait until then to inform the father."

"So you're keeping the baby?" He lifted one brow.

"Yes." There, it was out. And now that Sebastian believed I was having another man's baby, there was no way he'd be attracted to me in any way. Zero chance of anything happening there. My gaze darted toward the kitchen. "Can I have a glass of water before I take off?"

"Let me get that for you." He set his guitar on the sofa and flicked a hand in the direction of the kitchen. Apparently, I was supposed to follow him.

"With or without ice, or do you prefer room temperature?" He grabbed a tall glass from a cabinet, then swiveled to face me.

How sweet of him to ask. Most guys didn't think of things like that. "Room temperature, please." I offered a small smile as my gaze followed him to a spout at the sink. He filled the glass and handed it to me. "Thanks." I took a gulp and set the glass down. "For the water and for taking care of me."

He shifted his weight and I could swear he was closer to me now. "The nap must've done you some good, because this is the first time I've seen you without a frown." He reached out an index finger and brushed the space between my brows. "You're even prettier now."

I peered up at him midgulp. Seriously? I knew he wasn't coming on to me. After how unpleasant I'd been, he couldn't possibly see me that way. He was probably just trying to encourage more good behavior. I vowed to stay nice, no matter how hard resentment toward him reared up and kicked me in the ass. I swallowed the last sip and handed him the glass. "Thanks."

A smiled played at the corner of his mouth as he took the glass from me. He set it on the counter behind me and his shoulder brushed mine. A billion little shivers danced along my skin and I drew in a breath. He closed the small space, leaning in toward my ear.

"What are you doing?" I asked, not daring to look at him. His face was much too close to mine.

"Experimenting."

I cleared my throat, hoping my voice sounded natural and unconcerned. "Well, experiment somewhere else. Go over there." I nodded toward the other side of the kitchen.

"Why don't *you* go over there?"

That was a very good question. I instinctively met his gaze, trying to figure out what the hell he was up to. But my brain started shutting down when I felt the hard muscles of his thighs against mine. "I was here first."

His smile widened and he used his thumb to

brush a stray hair off my cheek. "You're ridiculous, you know that? It's kind of cute how you pretend you're not mysteriously drawn to me."

I licked my lips. He was right. It didn't necessarily follow that he needed to know how right he was. For one thing, that would be humiliating. Second, if he returned even half the lust for me, we were in big, big trouble. I could still speak the truth without confirming his assumption. "Sebastian, I swear on my mother's grave that I absolutely do *not* like you."

He pressed his lips together and brought his other leg forward, bringing his body flush against mine. "I don't like you either. So what are we going to do about it?"

I flattened my palms against his stomach, but my brain somehow misfired and instead of pushing him away, my fingers splayed over his muscles. The pressure of his fingertips at my hips compelled me closer and I held my breath. No way would he kiss me. I mean, I was crabby, pregnant and hormonal. Plus, he'd outright admitted to not liking me. Not that I could blame him. Right now, any woman in a ten-mile radius had to be more attractive than me. So what was he up to?

I lifted my chin to meet his smoldering gaze, but my eyes drifted to his lips. He inched closer and I squirmed until I was up against the counter facing him. His hands skipped upward to press against my waist, then spread out as if they couldn't bear not to cover every inch of me. I hadn't been touched like that by a man since... well, since my drunken hook-up with Sebastian two months before. I melted against him, hooking the finger of one hand through his belt loop and the other sliding up his chest to wrap around his neck.

Keeping his gaze trained on me, he levered his hips against mine so slowly I could feel everything from his hip to the zipper on his pants. My mouth parted and his mouth crashed down on mine. I devoured the kiss with a hunger that consumed me. This was nothing like the kisses I'd had with him before. This was loneliness and need, betrayal and fear, all rolled up with a healthy dose of lust and hate. I stretched up on my tiptoes and my arms overlapped around his neck, squeezing him closer. Our tongues tangled and the craving for more burned through my soul.

He pulled back just enough to whisper against my lips. "I was right. You're like liquid fire."

But I hadn't been hot enough for him to remember me before, so why would I mean anything to him this time? My eyes stung and I dipped my head to avoid his gaze. I relaxed my grip on him and flattened my feet on the ground. Dropping my arms to my side, I went limp in his.

"Violet? What just happened? Where did you go?"

I laughed once, a harsh sound I didn't recognize. "Really, Sebastian? We don't even like each other." Turning, I angled my head away from him. My hair fell forward and hid my face. "This is a recipe for disaster. And don't forget I have a child to think about now. I need to stay focused."

He tunneled a hand through his hair, blew out a breath. "You're right. I'm sorry."

I should've known he'd give up so easily. And had he really just apologized for kissing me? My heart thudded louder, my pulse thundering in my ears. "I should get going." I circled back to the bedroom, grabbed my purse and shouted a goodbye, then swept over the stairs and down the short path to my car.

Cursing my twice-broken heart, I scolded myself for falling for him again. The first time, I'd been completely justified for judging him since he'd forgotten all about me. This round, he'd been fully aware of his every move. He wanted me and he had acted on it, but when I protested, he'd had the decency to pull back. Rather than push me to continue our make-out session or progress to his bedroom, he did the decent thing and admitted I was right. But I hated being right about us not being a good fit. I hated even more that he had agreed.

But that wasn't his fault. You feel what you feel and I couldn't fault him for it when he was actually a pretty good guy. Except for earlier in the evening when he'd been messing with my mind, he'd been gentlemanly, caring, and genuinely sweet. I knew he wasn't the loser I'd tried to make myself believe him to be.

Or maybe our new connection growing inside me changed my views of everything. Maybe I saw what I wanted to see. Whatever, just because he was curious and wanted to experiment with me didn't mean he actually felt anything real for me. And why would I want him to? I'd already allowed our one night together to throw off my eight-year plan. I couldn't allow my infatuation with him to consume me for the next few months. He wasn't right for me. I needed to get that through my thick, red head.

At the stop sign, I wiped my tears and renewed my vow to lower my expectations when it came to Sebastian. I wanted so much more from a man — a real relationship. Sebastian would never get serious about me.

Unless he knew about the baby.

I had an inkling he would offer to do the "right" thing and then try to make it work with me for the baby's sake. The thought of him entering into a pity relationship and not truly loving me made me want to vomit. Not wanting to drive with my emotions going haywire, I pulled over to the curb.

I couldn't tell Sebastian he was the father, not for a while anyway. All I could do was get to know Sebastian and see where we went. Oh, Lord, I was all over the place. I'd told myself over and over that I didn't want him, but then I got angry and frustrated with him for not returning my feelings.

If I were to be brutally honest with myself, I'd already fallen for Sebastian that night two months ago. And getting to know him as a sober man only deepened my feelings. My bitterness toward him now was simply that of a scorned lover. Well, I'd just have to get over it, let the humiliation and bitterness go. Because if I didn't, having a baby with him would be so much more difficult. And I didn't need the extra stress.

I had the next several weeks to create some kind of foundation with Sebastian and get over myself. Our baby needed his dad. Sebastian could completely change his mind when faced with reality and decide to opt out of the baby's life. But I refused to be the cause of that choice. From now on, I'd find the will to forgive him. Whatever inappropriate and impractical affection I had for Sebastian, I'd redirect to the baby.

My hollow heart gradually filled with love for my baby as I dreamed of a happy life for him. Or her. I just had to forget the past and my gross lapse of judgment with Sebastian, and get through my infatuation with him. And since I didn't have anything scheduled for Sebastian for two or three days, I had time to regroup and get my head together.

I could do this.

CHAPTER NINE
★ Sebastian ★

The next afternoon, I sat in bed with my laptop and couldn't get Violet out of my mind. Or her long, red curls and her green eyes, and especially those soft, plump lips. I scrolled through her premade tweets, squashing the urge to create some of my own. It was *my* Twitter account, *my* life. Why did I have to do every little thing she told me to? I was a grown man and had been thinking for myself since I'd turned eighteen and bailed from my parents. Aside from the last three years of partying hard, I'd done okay. I was sober now. I could handle myself again.

But if I did anything publicly that veered off Violet's plan, she'd be all over me. Hell, she'd probably drive all the way to my house to chew me out. I didn't want her to make an extra effort if she was too tired. On the other hand, if she was too tired to leave my house, she'd be forced to stay.

We didn't have any PR activities planned for a few days, which meant I wouldn't be seeing her until we attended whatever event was next on her list... unless I did something that forced her to come over.

Though I suspected I'd regret it somehow, I composed a tweet, attached a picture and clicked the send button. I wondered how long it would take for her to notice.

By the time I'd entered the last of my recent lyrics into the computer and emailed them to Liam, twenty minutes had passed. Just as my stomach began to growl, my phone dinged and I checked the screen. Violet had sent me a text: *You'd better be home because I'm on my way.*

I snickered and strolled into the kitchen to take out the steaks I'd been marinating, unlocking the door for Violet on my way. No woman had ever turned down one of my steaks.

But first, tea. I plopped some ginger shavings into a pan of water to simmer on the stove.

Once I turned on the flame under two skillets, I chopped fresh thyme and garlic, then diced several potatoes and poured it all into a skillet. The pan sizzled and I lowered the flame. After I chopped the lettuce, I added cherry tomatoes, dried cranberries and a mix of walnuts, pecans and pumpkin seeds. Then I made up the dressing with balsamic vinegar, olive oil and maple syrup. I tossed the ingredients together and set the salad in the fridge to chill.

Just before I was about to throw the steaks on, I went out to the garden and picked some red peonies, pink phlox, white asters and a few black-eyed Susans, then floated them in a shallow glass bowl of water, silently thanking my gardener. I set the bowl in the middle of the dining room table, then threw the two steaks into the skillet and turned down the heat. I laid out the flatware, steak knives, salt and pepper shakers, and napkins on the table.

When I lifted the lid to check the tenderness of the asparagus, a knock sounded at the door. "Come in!"

She did just that, storming in and practically coming to a screeching halt as she inhaled deeply. "What's that smell?"

She couldn't find out I'd set her up. "Steak and potatoes. There's plenty if you're hungry." I sliced some lime wedges and placed them on the edge of a mug, then drizzled in some maple syrup. I poured the boiling water, careful not to let the ginger slivers fall into the cup. I handed it to her.

"What's this?"

"Ginger tea. It's good for upset stomachs."

She just stared at me, then slowly set the mug down, her brows wrinkling in the middle. "What are you up to?"

I lifted one shoulder. "I'm hungry, so I thought I'd throw on a steak and salad. Then I decided to fry up some potatoes. After you texted that you were on your way, I figured I should make sure there's enough for you too, since it's rude to eat in front of others. And people usually like liquids with their meals, thus the ginger tea."

She blinked, watching me flip the steak over. "Maybe I'm not hungry."

"It's all the same to me." After scooping up a helping of the potatoes and heaping them on the plates, I lifted a corner of the steak while peering at her over my shoulder. "How do you like your steak?"

Her eyes glazed over as she ogled the food. "Medium."

"Great. This one's yours." I plucked it out of the pan and laid it on one of the plates, while I let the other steak cook a little more. I carried the plate to the table, grabbing the bowl of salad on my way. I darted back into the kitchen for something to use to serve the salad, settling on a giant spoon. Using it to stir it a bit more to freshen up the dressing on the lettuce, I scooped up a bunch and set it on her plate.

I dashed back into the kitchen, dragged my own steak onto the plate, then headed back to the table. "Have a seat and dig in," I told her.

She hesitated, remaining standing as her fingers curled over the back of the chair.

I took my first bite of the steak and my eyes nearly rolled to the back of my head. "Mm."

Violet slid the chair out and sat, glancing at me before scooting the chair in. "You didn't set this up?"

"Do you mean is there some sinister plot to feed you?" I chuckled. "You should eat before it gets cold."

She snatched the knife at her side and carved a small piece from the steak. As soon as the meat hit her mouth, she moaned and began to chew. "Oh, my God," she said as she cut another piece. "What do you have in here, crack? It's amazing."

I grinned and scooted the mug toward her. "Don't forget the tea."

She shot me a suspicious glance, but as soon as she returned to her plate, I was long forgotten. Watching her enjoy her food with such intensity warmed me, made me feel more whole than I had in three years. I immediately began plotting a way to get her over for dinner tomorrow.

"So what's the deal with the baby's father? What's he like?" I asked, taking another bite of my own steak.

Her head bobbed side to side as she finished chewing. "I don't know him very well. At first glance, one might think he's a bit on the wild side, but I think deep down he might be a pretty good guy."

Jealousy wormed its way into my head and I pushed it away. I had no rights over Violet or her baby. I didn't want those rights and I didn't even like Violet.

Okay, maybe I did. A little. Between my urge to wrap her hair around my hand and yank her against me and my desire to get my tongue in her mouth again, it was hard to tell what I felt, other than lust.

"Do you see him much?" I asked, trying to act like I was making casual conversation instead of fishing for information on my competition.

"I've seen him a few times since the incident."

I laughed. "You mean when he knocked you up?"

She nodded, as she salted her potatoes. "This is so good."

"Do you like him?"

She drew in a long, shaky breath. "Sometimes. I'm not sure I should though. He's not the kind of guy I imagined myself having children with."

I muscled through the desire to find out who this guy was and mark my territory. Maybe having Violet over had been a bad idea. Instead of helping me through whatever this was, I found myself wanting her more. I wanted to show her why she should consider me as a better option than some guy who got her pregnant and who probably didn't want her half as much as I did.

I was getting way ahead of myself. Seriously, I barely knew her. "Your tea. Drink."

She rolled her eyes, but downed the rest of it. "That's pretty tasty, actually. You used fresh ginger, didn't you? Will you tell me how to make it?"

"Yeah. You're supposed to add lime and honey. Except I used maple syrup instead, because some people believe honey is bad for pregnant women."

Her eyes narrowed again. "You researched this for me?"

"Definitely not. I remember Faith mentioning something about being careful with honey when she was pregnant. Could be a myth, but I figured better to be on the safe side."

"Thank you. It was really lovely." Her smile lit up her eyes and my heart thumped louder. What was it about her that drew me in?

She pushed her plate away and leaned back. "I can't remember the last time I ate something that good."

"I was going to make a cappuccino, if you'd like one. I have some organic decaf, so you don't have to worry about it keeping you up tonight." I grabbed her plate and layered it over my own. "Maybe a little chocolate on top?"

"It sounds unbelievable." She sighed. "Careful or I'll be showing up every day to eat." She laughed as if it were a joke. Little did she know... "Need some help?" she asked.

I glanced at her over my shoulder as I set out the coffee and turned on my espresso machine. "Not really. It's a one-man job."

She leaned against the stove about a yard away. "So let's talk about the Fat Boy post on Twitter."

I raised one brow at her. "You mean the motorcycle."

"Whatever. We agreed you'd only use the posts I gave you."

Fortunately, I'd already prepared a response. "It's a motorcycle, Violet. Just a motorcycle."

"No." She shook her head. "In your case, it's only *just* if it's a puppy or a house. But motorcycles won't help your rep, not right now. They don't exactly scream stable or tame."

I stopped the machine at about a shot, then began steaming the milk. After adding milk to the cup, I spooned in foam, then sprinkled chocolate on tip. Taking a toothpick, I moved the powder over the foam until it looked like a tree. I grabbed a matching saucer, and slid it and the mug along the counter until it was next to her and I was inches away. "Hey, it's just a motorcycle," I said softly. "And I can't be limited to those tweets. They're not me and you can only do that so long before people figure out it's fake. You gotta let me put some of myself into whatever I'm supposedly saying."

She squeezed her eyes shut and began shaking her head. "We can't take the chance that you're going to say something crazy, something that undoes all our hard work."

"Like what? Tell them I worked out today, or what I bought at the grocery store? Boring crap like that? Or I could invite them in, show them a picture of a motorcycle I like or tell them how I made dinner for a beautiful woman."

"Stop." She pressed her fingertips to her forehead. "You're getting off track."

I peeled her fingers from her face. "Hey, I won't screw it up. I promise."

Before I had a chance to think better of it, my fingers had already tangled with hers. I let my thumb take control for an instant and brush across her soft skin. "I'm not going to screw it up," I repeated. "Those days are over."

She disentangled herself from me, then grabbed the cup and brought it to her lips with both hands. "This cappuccino is unbelievable. Perfect." Her lids fluttered as she savored another swallow. "They say the craving for alcohol never goes away, that you're always in danger of slipping."

"For some people, it's a daily struggle to stay sober, I suppose. Not for me." I started the faucet to get the water hot.

"What makes you different?" She took another slurp from the rim of the mug, peering up at me from under her lashes.

"Because I don't crave it, never did. I don't even like the taste. I just used it as a temporary blinder to put me in a place where I didn't have to care about anything." I turned around and rinsed the dishes, then loaded them in the dishwasher. "Now that I'm clean, I just can't seem to work up the desire to kill brain cells again."

Violet moved to my side and into my line of vision, wrinkling her nose. "Are you sure you're not just in denial? That you're not going to lose it one day and hit the bottle?"

I laughed. "Positive."

She chewed her bottom lip, glancing away. "Well, thanks for dinner. I should probably go."

I shrugged, trying not to care. "I was going to work on the interview questions for Alternative Magazine. Sure you don't want to backseat drive me on that?"

Her mouth curved up. "Of course I want to. But I have internet, you know. You can send it to me before you email it to them."

"Where's the fun in that? You have something better to do?" I smiled and waited a beat. "Want me to microwave some popcorn?"

"Look, Sebastian..."

Oh, here it comes. "What?"

"What's your deal?" She worried her lip again, making me want to nibble on it, too. "Why am I here?"

I grinned and reached into the cupboard to grab a bag of popcorn. I stuffed it into the microwave and hit the Popcorn button. "Because I don't like you."

She did her best to hide her grin as she slid onto the stool at the counter. "Okay, while you're not liking me, melt some butter for that, would you?"

"Sure thing." I grabbed a saucepan and dropped a cube in it, my heart skipping a beat as I turned the heat to low. "By the way, studies show that if you exercise, like take daily walks, and up your water intake, you can raise your energy level. Might not tire out so quickly." I snuck a peek at her and wondered if I'd gone too far.

She froze, then swallowed, her eyes watering. "Uhm..."

"What?" I shuffled over to stand on the other side of the counter. "Should I not give sound advice, something that might help you?" Loud pops sounded from inside the microwave but I ignored it, my attention fixed on Violet's reaction.

Violet shook her head. "No. I'm just not totally comfortable when you're all nice and everything."

"Well, then." I wagged a finger at her. "No popcorn for you. Sorry." I found a big bowl and set it in front of the microwave, then turned off the burner under the butter.

She chuckled. "You like cooking?"

"I enjoy creating music above anything, but I love eating good food. When I gave up drugs and alcohol, I had this powerful urge to quit everything else bad and, for me, that includes most restaurant food. I work out nearly every day for at least an hour, usually more. It would be stupid if I went through all that effort, then put garbage food in my body." The tiny explosions in the microwave stopped almost completely and I retrieved the bag, careful to not get burned. I cut the top and poured it into the bowl, then drizzled the butter over it and sprinkled in salt.

She dove for the popcorn as soon as I set it in front of her. "But somehow popcorn made the cut for this new, all-healthy way of life?"

I laughed. "I'm not a fanatic. I eat healthy when I can, but every now and then I want something junky. Fortunately for us both, this popcorn is organic."

"You know, aside from that lunch with my dad, I think that was the first decent meal I've had in a while." She tossed a single popcorn into her mouth, eyeing me. "That was sweet of you to manipulate me. Thank you."

She'd nailed me. But she didn't seem upset about it. "My pleasure. Except that I really was hungry. Good timing on your part."

Violet yawned and her eyelids drooped slightly. I needed to let her go, at least for tonight. On the upside, since we didn't get a chance to work on the interview today, I could use it as an excuse when I lured her over tomorrow.

Several minutes later, I walked Violet to her car, but I lagged behind, knowing if I got any closer, I'd want to kiss her. I didn't want to spook her. She arrived in front of the Lexus door and abruptly turned. "You know, I dislike you more today than I did yesterday," she said.

"Keep this up and I'll downright hate you by next week." I gave her a half laugh.

One side of her mouth curled up and she waved before climbing into her car and driving away.

Damn. Though I was fully aware that I couldn't be in love with Violet, it sure felt like I was well on my way to getting there. What was it about this girl that made me want to take care of her — and then toss her on the bed and show her how much I wanted her?

CHAPTER TEN
★ *Sebastian* ★

My hands clamped around the pole on the salmon ladder. I swung my legs to build momentum, then I jumped the pole onto the next rung. And then I moved it up three more rungs. As I was putting away the pole, my phone pinged. My heart rate picked up, hoping it was Violet. But I wasn't going to quit my exercise routine in hopes that she had texted me. The moment I dropped everything for a girl was the moment I was whipped. And I refused to be whipped by a girl who I seriously doubted was genuinely interested in me. Okay, so she'd kissed me the other day. But then she'd put the brakes on. So why should I jump every time my cell phone alerted me of a text?

I wiped the sweat off my hands and eyed my phone sitting on the shelf just two yards away. And then suddenly, I was holding my phone and typing in the password Violet had insisted I lock my phone with.

Ah, hell. I was whipped.

But it wasn't Violet texting me. It was Liam saying he loved the lyrics I'd emailed him. I shot off a quick reply and got on the treadmill, wondering what I'd make for dinner later.

What the hell was wrong with me, chasing after a woman who was pregnant with another man's child? I was seriously and severely mentally challenged. With my luck, she'd resolve things with the father and end up marrying him. I'd be the dumbass wanting what I could never have, what I should never have tried for in the first place.

Yet I *had* to try.

For the life of me, I couldn't figure out why Violet had been so bitchy when we'd first started this project. But she wasn't like that at all anymore. I had no idea what changed or why. All I knew was how I felt when I was around her. When she was near, all my past failures fell away. When I was with her, I felt hope that I could be happy again one day. Maybe. I didn't think about my horrible parents or how much I missed my sister. I just felt good. And I wanted more of that.

I finished running four miles on the treadmill and grabbed a towel. As I patted my neck and chest, my phone taunted me. I stared at it another minute, then gave up and made a beeline for it, finding Violet's text thread and added, *Come over and help me with the interview? There's some creamy Cajun chicken pasta in it for you.*

I tapped the phone against the ball of my hand, too antsy to do anything else. A minute passed and still no return text. Damn it. I was a moron. Shouldn't have pushed. I tossed my cell onto the sofa on my way to the fridge for some ice-cold water. Just as I started filling the glass, my phone dinged from the other room. I slammed down the cup and rocketed to my phone.

What time? Violet asked.

My face split with a huge grin. *Six o'clock?*

I need to be home early. Make it five and it's a deal.

Great. See you then. Yes! I fist-pumped and chucked my phone back onto the sofa. I had two hours to make a mouth-watering creamy Cajun chicken pasta. And a salad, of course. The baby needed vegetables.

But Violet's stomach probably didn't need unnecessary aggravation. I should go lighter on the spices, and make up for it in cheese.

I jogged into the kitchen and got out my spices: white pepper, garlic powder, onion powder, cayenne pepper, paprika and black pepper. Then I took out some butter to soften for the garlic bread.

An hour and forty-five minutes later, I had showered and dinner was nearly ready. After I set out my laptop with my interview questions open on the screen, I texted her with *Door's unlocked* and then I set the table. I cut the french bread and slathered the slices with garlic butter, then laid them on a cookie tray and preheated the oven. As I drained the noodles, the door creaked open.

"Sebastian?"

"In the kitchen," I shouted.

She came into view, her nose in the air. "Dear God. That smells incredible. You're ruining me, you know."

My mouth almost dropped open. She'd put makeup on and the green in her eyes popped against the pink in her sweater. "Can't go wrong with getting used to good, healthy food. Hungry?"

She rested her elbows on the counter bar. "I am *now*. You know, if that tastes as good as it smells, I'm *really* not going to like you."

I leaned over the counter, slipped my fingers behind her neck and made sure I had her attention before saying, "I'm liking you less and less by the minute."

She blinked and I was pretty sure she was holding her breath. Probably wondering if I was going to attempt another kiss. Well, I totally planned that in the near future, but not yet. I'd see if I could get *her* to initiate our next kiss. I spun around and slid the garlic bread into the broiler. "Give it three or four minutes and we're good to go."

"If food wasn't going to be ready until five-oh-five, why did you tell me to be here at five?" She rolled her eyes. "Geez, you really make a girl work for it."

I didn't bother hiding my smile. "So you're workin' it for me, are you?"

Violet tapped her bottom lip. "Hm. Trick question. If I answer no, I might not get fed. If I answer yes, that'll get me into more trouble than starvation. I'm going to take the fifth."

"That'll have to do." I liked her new attitude with me and was beginning to think this was the real Violet. Which led me to... "So, I have to ask. Why were you so mad at me when we first started this project?"

The light went out of her eyes and I immediately regretted bringing it up. "Let's just say that I thought you were someone else. But I'm beginning to see that you're not that person at all."

"That's a relief. Maybe one day you'll trust me enough tell me about that person you thought I was, and why." I watched her fidget and knew I had to drop it. "Until then, it's time to eat. Go sit and I'll bring it to you."

Her smile returned and she moved to the dining room table. I pulled the garlic bread from the broiler, served up the chicken Cajun pasta, gave her a generous portion of salad and tossed a piece of garlic bread on her plate, then set it in front of her. Her eyes sparkled and my insides warmed knowing my food put that glow on her face. I wanted to feed her and the baby every single day. Especially since

I didn't have many better things to do until Full Throttle started touring again.

I fixed my own plate and sat across from her. "What made you decide to get into public relations?"

"I like shaping someone's image and helping them with their career." A forkful of pasta hovered near her mouth. "Though I don't particularly like celebrities — no offense — I like the business. And I'm really good at it, manipulating the media and all that. I kind of geek out on that kind of thing."

"No other passions? You're not a closet actress or anything?"

She laughed. "Hell, no. I'm not very artistic in that way. I'm better at figuring things out, solving problems." She loaded up her fork again. "By the way, the extra water I drank and the power walk this morning helped. Not as energetic as before the baby came along, but it's definitely better."

"That's great. And the nausea?" I shoved a bite of pasta in my mouth.

"Better, thanks. It seems to be settling down a bit." Violet darted glances at me while she swirled the fork in her pasta mound. "I'm curious. Did you go to college or anything or did you skip all that in favor of your music?"

"College wasn't an option, not really." I stared down at my plate, suddenly no longer hungry. "My parents didn't have the money for tuition, or so they claimed, and my grades weren't good enough for a scholarship. I spent most of high school too stressed out, hoping I wasn't going to get my ass beat that day, while praying it would be me and not my sister, India."

She was silent a long moment as she broke off a piece of garlic bread. "What did you do instead of college?"

"I became a short order cook." I waved a hand between my plate and hers. "That's where I got some of my mad skills. I've been experimenting ever since."

"Ever thought about opening your own restaurant? Because this is *really* good." She closed her eyes. "I mean, seriously. I'd totally eat at your restaurant. Probably every day."

I laughed. "Maybe up the road. Right now, it's all about my music career. It'll always be my first love."

Her fingers stilled around the fork and I wondered what I'd said wrong. "Always? Like, over wife and family?"

I scoffed, digging into my food again. "Of course not. If I had a kid..." And that possibility was quite real, since I had so little memory of one or two of drinking binges. "He or she would be my number one priority. And my wife, of course."

She speared a few pieces of baby lettuce and a

cherry tomato, then met my gaze again. "So you actually *want* to get married one day?" She shook her head. "I don't know why I'm asking. It's just that you're, what, twenty-five? Most guys your age aren't interested in being in a serious relationship."

My stomach full, I nudged my plate aside. "I've crammed a lot into these last three years and I'm done with relationships that go nowhere. I have a future now. For the first time in my life, I realize that and I don't want to do it alone. Especially when I see how happy Liam and Emma are. Makes me want that too."

For the life of me, I couldn't figure out why her eyes were pooling. Had I said something wrong again? "You okay?"

"Yes. Dinner was wonderful." Her smile was a bit too bright, but I didn't want to push. "We should probably get started on that interview. I guess you never know when I'm going to get tired and need to go."

Great, she'd shut down again. But at least she hadn't gone back to being mean. "Hey, whatever I said to upset you, I'm sorry."

Her eyes turned on like a faucet and I could've have punched myself. Why did I have to open my mouth again?

She gave a watery laugh. "It's not you, I promise. It's the stupid hormones. I'm pretty sure I'm at an all-time high on crazy."

My shoulders loosened and I cleared our plates from the table. "Faith was on the emotional rollercoaster for a few months. Not everyone is the same though. Could be less for you."

She opened her mouth to talk, but the front door creaked.

"Sebastian?"

What was Liam doing here? I deposited the plates on the counter and made my way to the living room to see Liam holding hands with Emma, his fiancée. His free arm held Emma's daughter, Scarlet. Liam's sister Faith was with them, her son Xander attached to her hip.

"What brings you guys here?" I asked, drying my hands on the kitchen towel.

"Hadn't heard much from you the last few days," Liam said, glancing at Emma, then his sister. "Thought we'd pass by on our way to dinner and check up on you."

Sebastian shrugged. "Works for me. Everyone know Violet?"

"Violet, so nice to finally meet you." Emma ambushed her into a warm hug. "You did wonders for Liam's rep."

"The media hasn't been joking about me being Saint Nick, so I'm happy." Liam bent forward and bussed Violet's cheek. "What are you doing hanging out with this bozo after business hours?"

She flashed him a mischievous smile. "I'm just in it for the food."

Faith chuckled and pulled Violet into a hug. "Good to see you again. We need to hang after you're done fixing up Sebastian."

"I'd love to." Violet motioned toward the dining room chairs. "Did you guys want to sit? You might get lucky and Sebastian will feed you."

If Liam and Emma stayed, maybe Violet would also stay and hang out with us. I'd get more time with her. And if we didn't get to the interview tonight, I could probably talk her into coming over tomorrow. I'd get another day with her. "You can get food here a hell of a lot faster than if you drive somewhere, order and then wait. I have plenty of chicken and sauce. Just have to cook up more noodles."

"As if I'd say no to your cooking." Liam punched Sebastian in the arm.

Xander screeched and Faith sprung from her chair. "Mind if I get the emergency toys?"

"That's why I bought them." I filled up the pan to boil the noodles and listened to my guests chatter. While Violet filled Liam in on the progress of her program, Faith and Emma kept the kids occupied. And my heart sang because Violet was still there. Yep, whipped. Totally.

I fixed everyone a plate, including the kids. As I served each person, Violet's gaze followed the plates. I made her another one, smaller this time. She grinned as I placed it in front of her, and then she dove in. "I'm beginning to really hate you now."

"Feeling's mutual." I grinned.

Everyone finished eating and Violet didn't rush off. The girls huddled near the kids and I grabbed my guitar, figuring Liam and I could jam a bit. Xander rushed me and I moved the guitar aside so he could climb into my lap. I positioned the guitar in front of him. "Just like last time, I'll handle the part at the end and you brush the strings."

Xander got his hand ready and I hit the first chord for *Mary Had a Little Lamb*. In my peripheral vision, Violet participated in an animated conversation with Faith and Emma, but every now and then, she glanced over at us. I wondered what she was thinking, how long she'd stick around.

A few minutes later, a shadow covered the guitar and Faith bent over to muss Xander's hair. "It's way past your bedtime, buddy. We gotta go."

"Scarlet's bedtime too." Emma scooped up her daughter and threw her on a hip.

Hugs made the rounds and they filed out, leaving Violet and me alone again.

"I really should go too. Probably shouldn't have had the second helping. All my energy is going toward digesting it." She put a hand over her mouth while she yawned.

Damn. "I'll walk you out."

Just like the night before, I slowed as she neared her car. Otherwise, I'd be tempted to swoop. I stuffed my hands in my jeans pocket to ward against the chilly fall air. "Hey, what sounds good for dinner tomorrow?" Risky move, but if she said no, at least I'd know that she didn't return my feelings and I'd have to keep them in check. I'd rather know now than weeks up the road after I was more invested.

"Surprise me." She beamed and spun to get into her car. Then she turned around again. "You should probably know that after that horrible dinner tonight, I'm well on my way to detesting you."

"Ditto." I flashed her a smile and waved as she got into her car and drove away.

CHAPTER ELEVEN

★ *Violet* ★

With nothing vital on my schedule for the day, I stayed in bed the next morning way longer than I should have. Images of Sebastian and the sweet way he played guitar with Xander enveloped me like a soft, warm blanket that didn't want to let me go. Before that, I'd been wondering if it was wise to see Sebastian again outside of work. But then I'd watched him with the kids and that had sealed the deal. What guy kept toys around the house for when his friends visited?

The good kind of guy.

I couldn't wait to have my first bite of whatever he prepared for dinner later today.

As I climbed out from under the covers, I felt like a total slacker. I hadn't slept well in weeks. Except the last two nights. And I had Sebastian to thank for finally being well rested. I'd gone to bed on a full yet settled stomach and had fallen asleep almost immediately. The nausea still teased me occasionally but thanks to the tea, I hadn't vomited in days.

I chugged some water, then grabbed my running shoes, slipped into some yoga pants and a tank top, then pulled on a sweatshirt. It was winter, after all. I had a few more gulps of water while I toasted some bread so I didn't get too hungry, then I brushed my teeth.

After grabbing my house key, I stuffed it in the tiny pocket of my yoga pants, clipped my cell phone on my waistband, then took a few more sips of my water and headed out the door. I locked up and walked down the long driveway to the sidewalk. The back of my neck tingled and I whirled around to see a girl in a black hoodie leaning against the fence and staring at me. Something about her brown eyes seemed familiar, called to me.

I watched her for a moment, wondering if she'd break eye contact with me, but she didn't. I'd heard stories about criminals using seemingly helpless girls to trap unsuspecting women or hijack their cars. But if she was genuinely in need..."Do you need help?"

"Yes." She didn't move, didn't even take her hands out of her pockets.

I quickly scanned the area, looking for a white van or anything suspicious. "How can I help?"

"I need information on Sebastian."

Crazed stalker fan? And how did she know I

knew him? How did she know where I lived? "How did you connect him to me?"

"You were on Periscope with him. You were also photographed with him recently at a restaurant. *The Dish* gave your whole name and I searched for everything about you that I could possibly find. Figured out you were Aidan Madison's daughter, found the address to his office, then followed him home."

My breath caught in my throat. She was either psychotic or desperate. Or both. "Why go through all that for info on Sebastian? I mean, you could always read up on him, like you did me, or find out if there's a small venue where he's appearing, talk to him at a Meet and Greet."

"If I meet him, I don't want a crowd." She shoved her hands deeper into her pockets. "But before I even think about that, I have some questions."

This was getting weirder and weirder. Instinct told me, though, she wasn't the average stalker, if she was a stalker at all. "Does Sebastian know who you are?"

She twisted her lips into a frown and her gaze dropped, her face disappearing into the hoodie. "Yes."

I softened my voice. "Before I tell you anything or arrange a meeting, I need to know who you are."

Her shoulders shifted, pulled back and she raised her chin to meet my gaze. "I'm his sister, India."

I gasped loud enough that the girl could hear

from several yards away, but she didn't seem fazed by it. Cool cucumber. "How do I know you're telling the truth?" As soon as she let the hoodie slide away, exposing her thick, dark hair, I saw the unmistakable resemblance to Sebastian. Identical smoky brown eyes, same thick wavy hair. She even had his face shape and skin coloring. And his stunning good looks. I cleared my throat. "Never mind."

"Will you help me?" she asked, her eyes silently begging me.

I rocked back on the heel of my sneakers, mulling over my options. She'd been on her own for three years and who knew where she'd been or what kind of a life she'd lived. Could I even trust her in my house?

"Hey, are you hungry? Maybe we can go out for a bite to eat. My treat." I smiled and started to head back toward the guest house for my purse.

She shook her head with vigor, the waves of her hair swishing against her shoulders. "I don't accept charity."

That was encouraging. At least I didn't have to worry about her trying to squeeze Sebastian for money. "I mooched a couple of dinners off Sebastian recently, so I could pay it forward. Someday, you can pay it forward too. I need to grab my purse." I vanished through my front door, snagged my purse, then darted back outside. She was still there. Whew!

"My car's this way." Without giving her a chance to say no, I made my way down the driveway toward the Lexus. I hit the fob and unlocked the door, jerking my head toward the passenger side.

She grabbed the door handle, then hesitated. "Is he a good guy?"

"Yeah, I think so." A slow smile spread over my face. "Actually, he's pretty great."

The lines between her brows disappeared and I was pretty sure she almost smiled. She got in the car and strapped herself in. "I feel bad for making you miss your workout."

"I have a light day. I'll do it later." I negotiated the Lexus out of the driveway and turned onto the street. "Any place in particular you'd like to eat?"

"Wherever." She turned away from me and silence filled the car.

I pulled into the parking lot of a nearby diner that I knew had good pancakes. And they served real maple syrup, not the corn syrup garbage restaurants usually served. I was totally craving the real thing after Sebastian had slipped it into the salad dressing and my tea.

India may have had questions for me, but I could probably see those questions and raise her a few more. But I held back. Sebastian would go crazy if he knew she was alive and in my car. If I said the wrong thing or asked the wrong question and she bolted, I'd never forgive myself. Neither would he.

Inside the restaurant and seated across from me, her eyes scanned the other patrons before zoning in on the menu.

"Do you have a place to live?" I asked.

She nodded. "Yeah."

I set my menu aside and locked gazes with her. "A *good* place? Are you safe?"

She blew out her breath in a long sigh. "I don't know how much information I want to give you, because I know you'll tell Sebastian and I haven't completely decided yet that I want to see him."

Though I didn't want to push, she'd opened the door and I couldn't resist. "Why wouldn't you want to see your brother?"

She scoffed. "He left me there with th-them."

"Your parents?"

"Yes." Tears filled in her eyes and she pressed a trembling fist to her mouth.

"Hi, I'm Winona and I'll be your server today." The plump brunette smiled. "Can I get you two anything to drink?"

"Coffee, please." I eyed India who didn't look like she was capable of speech. My heart ached for her. How awful their parents must have been to her and Sebastian. The fact that he wasn't thoroughly screwed up was probably a small miracle. I focused on the waitress. "Can you bring her some water until she decides?"

"Certainly." She pocketed her pad and pencil, and took off.

"So where have you been the last three years?" I had a feeling she wouldn't give me much. But maybe I'd get a tidbit, enough to know she wasn't in serious trouble.

"I haven't been on the streets or selling my body for drugs, if that's what you want to know. Before I ran away, I researched my options to see where I'd end up if I got caught. Did you know that you can get into trouble for harboring a runaway?"

"Ah." I nodded. "You don't want Sebastian to know who helped you, so they don't get into trouble."

Since India didn't comment on that and our conversation had stalled, I could use this time to put in a good word for Sebastian. "He told me your parents wouldn't let him see you. That by the time he got the paperwork together to try to get custody of you, you'd already disappeared. He searched all over for you. Two private investigators later, and he still couldn't find you."

India's face fell and she let out a whimper as her head slowly sunk toward the table until her forehead pressed against her wrists. The fabric of her hoodie muffled her sobs and I reached out my fingertips to stroke her hair and pat her quaking shoulders. She didn't flinch from me.

After a long moment, she sniffed and lifted her head. She dabbed her face with a napkin and gave a watery laugh. "I didn't know. I thought he'd abandoned me."

"No." I gave her hand a quick squeeze and withdrew. "He was devastated when he lost you."

She nodded and sucked in a deep, trembling breath then whispered, "I want to see him."

"I can take you directly to his place." My chest nearly burst with excitement for Sebastian and my own desire to reunite them. But India didn't seem totally stable and I didn't want to overwhelm her. Softening my voice, I kept it casual."Or we can wait. We can call first or just show up, however you want to play it."

"No. I have to be sure." She gnawed on a thumbnail, her eyes flitting around the room. "Someplace neutral. I want to be able to leave easily if I need to."

"Okay." The girl was jumpy and my nerves were wrecked from worrying if she was going to bolt at any moment. I was so close. "I could ask him to meet us here."

"No, too public." She patted her hoodie, making sure it was covering her head again.

I pursed my lips and searched my brain for somewhere she'd feel comfortable that wasn't public or his house. "Maybe after we eat, we could go back to my place and hang out. Watch some TV and relax. Have a snack later. You know, just chill until you're ready to see him. He can come to my house."

The waitress returned and India ordered orange juice and waffles. I went for the pancakes, my mouth watering so much I had to swallow in a hurry so I didn't spit on the table. The waitress pattered away and returned a moment later with India's orange juice, and topped off my coffee. I took a moment to open up the tiny containers of half and half and dump them in my cup. After a taste test, I refocused on India. "Well?"

"Okay."

My breath hitched. Unless India cleared out while I wasn't looking, Sebastian was about to meet his sister after three long and very qsad years.

CHAPTER TWELVE
★ *Sebastian* ★

I'd always loved answering fan mail. It could get tedious at times, like when I was busy on tour, but when I didn't have a lot going on, I loved talking to people. The weirdos were a different thing altogether. I moved all those emails to the "Psychos" folder and skipped to the next one. The normal fans were, after all, the reason I was a musician. What was the point in creating art or music without an audience? I wrote and played for them as much as for myself. Therefore, they were a part of my life. I *wanted* to talk to them.

My stomach growled and I hit the send button, shooting off an email to a teenager in Detroit. I closed my laptop, anxious to refuel, and my phone dinged. I dug it out of my pocket and checked the screen. Violet? I clicked on her name.

Want to come over for lunch?

Lunch, huh? I scratched my chin and stared at

the text. We hadn't made plans for today, other than dinner later. And if we got together before that, I had assumed I would be the one to initiate it. Well, I wasn't going to question my good fortune. *Good timing. I'm starving. Should I come over now?*

Okay.

I wasn't sure I appreciated the lack of enthusiasm in her text. But she wouldn't have invited me over if she didn't want to see me, right? Something was up. Bad news maybe? Some skank saying she was having my love child? I wouldn't find out unless I got my ass to Violet's house. I considered changing into something nicer than sweats, but that would take time. My stomach growled again, making the decision for me.

I grabbed my keys off the coffee table and headed out the door. Not wanting any paparazzi to find me so easily — thankfully they hadn't figured out my new address yet — I didn't take the Bugatti. Too high profile. I hopped into the Land Rover and headed out. Fifteen more minutes until food. What if she didn't have anything ready yet? Damn, I really should've had a snack before I left.

I parked the LR4 on the street in front of Aidan's, scanned the vicinity for suspicious activity — like my bandmates planning a prank — then got out of the car when nothing popped out as unusual. After strolling up the driveway, past the main house to her little house, I knocked.

She opened the door, then glanced over her shoulder, but didn't open it wide enough for me to come in. After another quick glance behind her, she opened the door a little wider. "Hey. Thanks for coming over." She chewed her bottom lip.

Since when did you thank someone for coming over for lunch? And Violet wasn't smiling. My bet was that she had an ulterior motive of some kind. This didn't bode well for my stomach. And why was the place closed up? The only light filtered through the thin fabric of the closed curtains. And as nearly as my nose could ascertain, there was nothing cooking on the stove. "This isn't about lunch, is it? What's going on?"

"Actually, pizza should be arriving in a few minutes. But I have to run out for a bit." She mashed her lips together, fidgeting and glancing again toward what was probably the door to her bedroom.

"You invited me over and now you're leaving?" I blocked the door before she could escape. "What's going on?"

Her whole body stilled, then she laid a hand on my chest, met my gaze and brought one hand up to cradle my face. "Do you trust me?"

I nodded, my stomach tightening. This was big, whatever she'd planned for me.

"Then let me go. I have some errands to run. Text me when you're ready for me to come back."

"Then I'd be texting you right now." She attempted to skirt around me and I clamped my fingers around her wrist. "So you leave and I just sit here and wait? Not even a hint as to why I'm here?"

"There's someone here to see you." She reached up on her tiptoes and brushed my lips with hers. "It's a good thing. Save me some pizza or I will shank you."

She slipped out the door, leaving me completely baffled. There was someone else in her house? I spun to see a small figure in the doorway. The hoodie slid down to rest on her neck and my lungs froze. My throat burned and I wasn't sure I could talk.

"Hey," she said.

Was this some kind of joke? Or was this really my sister? The silhouette of her hair and her figure both looked like she could be my India. But shadows covered her face. I wanted to walk to her and make sure, but my brain couldn't find my feet to send the command to move. My brain was really screwing up, because if this was India, my brain needed to tell my eyes that I wasn't sad. Yet they watered and I was afraid that if I got closer and looked into this girl's face, it wouldn't be her. And I'd lose her all over again.

"It's me. India." She took a hesitant step forward and the sun breaking through the microscopic holes of the drapes cast just enough light for me to see for myself.

Tears leaked from my eyes and my throat swelled too thick for air or anything else to pass through. "India," I croaked.

"Yeah, it's me." She closed the distance. Her chin quivered and her lashes clumped from tears.

"Oh, my God." I scooped her up by her tiny waist, lifting her into a hug and squeezing as I buried my face in her hair. "India."

I let myself go, weeping all over her and probably holding her way too tight, intent on never letting her go. Ever.

Minutes passed and we clung to each other. "I didn't know what happened to you. Thought I'd never see you again. I thought..." A small part of me thanked Violet for leaving and that she wouldn't see me become a blubbering mess. Not very manly. But the rest of me didn't care about anything other than being with my sister again.

My body went rigid. But was she really back? And for how long? Inch by inch, I loosened my hold on her. "So what now? You run off again, disappear?" I couldn't help the resentment creeping into my voice.

She leapt away from me, like she suddenly realized I had an infectious disease. The doorbell rang and I turned to get the door. Before I got there, she opened it and bolted. I almost smacked into the pizza guy. "Sorry, man." I slipped past him and caught up to India, snagging her hand and spinning her around.

"You were going to run again, without even giving me a chance?" I scoffed. "And you wondered why I was worried about you disappearing? Jesus." Still gripping her hand, I cursed under my breath, then focused on her again. I took the anger down a notch. I didn't want to drive her away. So I told her the truth, hoping that would be enough. "I couldn't take it if you left. It would destroy me."

"For a second there, I was back at home and Dad was angry at me." Tears sprang from her eyes and she shook her head. "I've been on the run a long time, and I reacted. But... I only just found you. I don't want to leave."

"Then don't." Gently this time, I squeezed her hand. "We'll swing by wherever your stuff is and then I'll take you home. My house. Or we can forget your things, forget that life ever existed, and I'll buy you all new stuff."

Her cheek fell onto my chest and she wrapped her arms around my waist. "I missed you so much. You have no idea."

I kissed the top of her head. "I'm pretty sure I do."

A throat cleared behind me. "Uhm, excuse me, where should I put the pizza?"

India gave him a watery laugh. "We should go

in and eat."

I slung my arm around her shoulder. "Yeah."

On the way back to the guest house, I relieved the delivery man of his two boxes. "Thank you," I told him, then I eyed India. "You guys better have ordered pepperoni."

She darted ahead of me to turn the door knob, then she paused and twisted with a smile. "I remember everything," she said softly.

I set the boxes on the counter, then pulled her in another hug. "I need you to stay."

"Okay."

I hoped that meant she wasn't going anywhere. As ravenous as I was, I let India get the first slice. "Was it hard on your own?"

She gave me a sad smile. "Only because I didn't have you."

I returned her smile. "But you were safe?"

She took the first bite of the slice but managed to answer. "I want to be bitter and tell you how much people suck. Because it's the truth. But there are so many good people out there. I had decent people looking out for me."

"You don't want to tell me who they are?" I dug into my pizza.

"They made me promise." She shook her head. "They were kind to me, treated me like I was their own. I'd never had that before. Except with you."

I chewed and swallowed. "I'm glad you had a safe place."

She grinned. "What's it like being a famous rock star?"

Sensing she didn't want to do the talking, I squashed my urge to ask her why she chose now to find me. I set the pizza down and wiped my hand on a napkin. "Strange. Fun. Stressful. Exciting."

She asked me questions faster than I could answer them, about the band and touring, while *not* talking about her life the last three years. We'd get to that eventually. Right now, I just wanted her to feel safe with me.

She wiped her mouth, tossed her crumpled napkin on the coffee table and shoved the pizza box away. "Four pieces left. We should save them for Violet."

"Speaking of which, we should probably let her into her own house." I leaned back in the chair, wondering if it was possible for a stomach to actually explode. Thankfully, I didn't have any photo shoots coming up where they would want to see my abs. "Do you mind?"

"If Violet's here?" She tipped her head to the side. "Why would I mind? She was super cool today."

I snatched my cell from next to the pizza box and texted her. *She wants to see you. Will you be home soon?*

I'm actually already here. Up front hangin' with my dad. Be right there.

I chuckled. "She's in the main house. So…" I flipped my cell from palm to palm. "You're coming to my house later to stay?"

"Won't having a teenager around all the time ruin your chances with the ladies?" She wiggled her eyebrows, then her face grew serious. "I don't want to cramp your style. And I don't want to be a burden. I can't stay with you if I'm always feeling like I owe you."

I snorted. "We're family. It's our job to take care of each other. I can't imagine you're going to want to lie around all day making messes and eating ice cream. That might be a problem for me eventually. But I don't think you'd be satisfied with that kind of life. Either way, there's no pressure to leave. Hell, we have three years to make up for."

A shaft of light flooded the place and I whipped around to see Violet coming in. She made a beeline for the pizza. "You losers better have saved me some."

I stood and held her by the shoulders, turning her until she faced me. Lifting her chin with my thumb, I bent toward her until our faces were only an inch away. Then my lips grazed hers, lingered for a moment before I straightened, my gaze holding hers.

Her lips curved up. "You're welcome," she whispered, then turned to India. "You're not leaving, right?"

India beamed. "I'm not going anywhere."

"Except with me," Sebastian said. "We should get going and not overstay our welcome."

Violet laughed softly. "I wouldn't mind the company."

That wasn't such a bad idea. Maybe she could squeeze some answers out of India. I switched to my sister. "Whatever you want to do."

"We don't have to rush off." India moved two slices of pizza onto a paper plate and handed it to Violet. Then she gathered up the used napkins and threw them in the kitchen trash.

"India, do you have a car?" Violet sunk into the couch and took a bite off the pizza.

"No, couldn't afford one." She perched on the arm of the sofa and I got comfortable in the chair where I could see them both.

Violet chewed and swallowed hurriedly. "When you tracked my dad and found me, how did you follow him without a car?"

"I borrowed a friend's," she said, fidgeting with the sleeve of her hoodie. "Except she didn't know I borrowed it. I filled up the tank though."

I chuckled. "That wasn't obvious," I joked.

Her brows knitted in the middle. "She didn't know it was me. But at least she knew the thief meant well."

"What made you choose today to see Sebastian?

Why now?" Violet bit off another chunk of pizza.

"I've been keeping tabs on him all along, even before he had Instagram and Facebook." India switched to me. "First, I was angry because you'd left me. Watched you get more famous, went to a live Full Throttle concert right around the time you guys won your Grammy. The last two years, every time you and your friends hit the news, it was all bad. And after growing up with *them* and the drugs and the violence, I vowed I wouldn't be anything like them. You'd become just like our parents and I refused to be around anyone like that."

I twitched. "I guess I can't deny it."

"Which is why I didn't try to contact you. Then suddenly you disappeared two months ago. When you reappeared last week you were everywhere all at once, but you seemed different. Then I read about you going into rehab."

I'd been so torn up about her disappearance that I'd hit the bottle, but the very reason she'd stayed away was because I'd been drinking. I'd lost all that time with my sister, because I'd been feeling sorry for myself. If I hadn't been so pathetic, she might've come back to me sooner.

I scrubbed my hands over my face, wishing I could undo the last three years. "I'm sorry." I dropped on the couch next to her. "I'm so sorry."

"Not like I can blame you." She joined her hands

with mine. "You had eighteen years with those toxic people. I only had fifteen and most of that time, you were taking the beatings for me. It was messed up, but it's over. We're together again and they're out of our lives."

"So what happened to Dad?"

Her gaze drifted to the carpet. "An injury, followed by painkillers."

"I remember the back surgery. There's gotta be more to the story." I nudged her knee. "What else?"

"After a while, the painkillers weren't enough. He moved on to harder stuff, like cocaine. He died of a heroin overdose. He just stopped breathing."

A sick feeling festered in my gut. "And he got Mom hooked?"

"Looks that way," she whispered. "She's still in the same house. I have no idea how she manages the mortgage payment without Dad. I think she makes meth."

I groaned as the last shred of hope died that my mother would pull herself out of her own hell. "Last time I passed by the house, I assumed they'd sold it and someone else had moved in. There was all kinds of junk in the yard and a window was boarded up. I couldn't imagine they would live in a dump like that."

India grimaced. "And yet they did."

"I wish I had figured out a way to get you."

"You couldn't do anything, I see that now." Air rushed out of her lungs and her shoulders slumped. "By the time I realized they were getting worse, you'd stopped coming around and they'd taken my phone. I didn't have your phone number anymore."

"I stopped coming around, because Dad threatened me. Rather than fight with him, I put all my energy into taking the legal route. But I was too late and you left before I could get custody of you." I paused, remembering the burning frustration. "After you disappeared, I hired two private investigators to find you, but you'd made sure no one could. I don't blame you."

India laid a hand on my arm. "Violet says you're done with drinking. Is that true?"

I raised my right hand. "I swear on my life."

"Can we stop by my friend's house and pick up my stuff?" India giggled. "She's a huge Full Throttle fan and has no idea we're related. She'll just die when she sees you."

CHAPTER THIRTEEN

★ *Violet* ★

Adrenaline had rushed through my veins since I'd first seen India earlier this morning and my nerves had held me captive since then. But I'd done it. I'd reunited Sebastian with his sister without her running away. It was over now though, and cell by cell, my body returned to normal. As I watched India and Sebastian get gradually closer, the old wounds healing over, I realized I was losing a piece of Sebastian. What had begun between us and might've had the chance to grow into something deeper would likely fizzle over the next few days. He had India back.

Granted, a sister couldn't take the place of a love interest. But she would fill that hole in him that had been drilled into his heart three years ago. And he'd likely be busy over the next few days, reconnecting and getting her settled in. Between that and my list of appearances, he wouldn't have time for spontaneous dinners. A darkness settled over me at the thought of missing Sebastian.

As they chatted by the door, I sidestepped out of their view and wiped my eyes. Damn hormones.

"Violet, where did you go?" He popped his head past the wall, his eyes narrowing. "Are you okay?"

I managed a watery smile. "Emotions running amok. Sorry."

"You should come with us to get her stuff. Hang out for a while, have dinner later. Then I'll drive you home."

I scraped the toe of my sneakers on a speck on the floor. "I should get ahead of my work. Otherwise, I'll be panicked to keep up with everything. Besides, you two need some time together."

"We have the rest of our lives for that." India tugged on my hand. "You're coming with us."

Since I probably wouldn't have much time with him the next few weeks, how could I say no? Sebastian reached for me, his thumb brushing the fleshy part of my hand. He smiled and that was all I needed. My chest expanded, filled, and at that moment, I would've gone anywhere with him. "Sure."

India's friend lived in Hemet. Fatigue from an already long day snuck into my feet and up my legs, making me drag a little. Instead of enjoying the drive, I nodded off. "You guys go in without me," I said once the car stopped. "I'm still waking up."

Before he killed the engine, he cracked the window. "I'll help her pack and get back faster."

She peered over at her brother. "I packed before I left, just in case."

He grinned before walking her down the pathway to the front door. Instead of India going right in, she held up her hand for him to wait, then she knocked on the door. My guess was that she wanted to surprise the resident Full Throttle fan. An instant later, a cute black girl poked her head out the door. Recognizing India, she stepped outside onto the porch. I couldn't make out what they were saying, but I could see the girl's eyes widen when she looked at Sebastian. She covered her mouth as she squealed and began to jump up and down. I definitely heard the screaming, even from the distance.

India darted inside, leaving her friend on the porch with Sebastian. I only saw the back of his head and she didn't open her mouth much. He was probably doing most of the talking. She stared at him wide eyed, nodding occasionally. Several minutes later, India emerged with two suitcases. The girl handed India a cell phone and Sebastian pulled the girl into a hug while India aimed the phone at them.

No one was forcing him to be so nice to his fans. He could have smiled, given the minimal time that would make him appear the least rude and be on his way. Instead, he gave them what they wanted, just a few extra moments that made their day. And after that display of sweetness, I was officially on the edge, this-close to totally and completely falling for Sebastian.

But I couldn't let my unchecked emotions cloud my judgment. The baby would grow quickly and in just a few months, I'd be huge. Sebastian wasn't in love with me and I seriously doubted he could get past the extra weight from a baby he believed belonged to someone else.

Even if he cared more for me than I believed, emotions had zero impact on long-term survival. We were too different in all the important ways. Sebastian may have been sweet, over-the-top sexy and incredibly talented, but he had barely made it through high school and he couldn't compete with me cerebrally any more than I could compete with him in music.

I needed a guy who could keep up in the ways that mattered to me and I absolutely, without a doubt, had no intention of taking up with a celebrity.

Today would be our last day associating in a nonprofessional way. I'd hang out with him and his sister for a little while, then he'd take me home. He'd make up for the three years without India and catch up with her. I'd return to my own life, comfortable with the fact that our child had two loving parents. A few weeks up the road when our new and business-only relationship falls into an easy routine, I'll tell him about the baby. In the meantime, I had today and I intended to enjoy it.

He wrapped his arms around the girl again, dropped a kiss on her forehead, then wrestled both suitcases from India and headed toward me. That was above and beyond. And I didn't think he was being extra nice to the girl to impress his sister. Sebastian really was that caring.

I took a deep breath and muscled through the desire to ignore my head and do whatever the hell I wanted. I couldn't let myself go, though. It wouldn't be fair to Sebastian to allow our relationship, whatever it was, to continue on this course when I had no intention of making it any kind of permanent.

Sebastian opened the back and they loaded her luggage, then they climbed into the car. India's face appeared between my seat in front and Sebastian's, her grin spreading wider. "Did you see her face? That was crazy!"

I laughed. I'd known India only a few hours and already adored her. My fingers touched my stomach, and gratitude filled me that my child would be able to call this wonderful girl Auntie.

★

I had a nice time at Sebastian's house with him and India, but much of their conversation revolved around their past, people they knew and a few funny stories. The anecdotes never involved their parents. India and Sebastian never said one positive word about them.

Though my mother had passed away, I'd always had a strong bond with her and when I'd moved in with my dad, we'd struggled over some pretty big rocks in the road. But he'd never been cruel and through it all, I knew he cared. Sebastian and India had never had that safety net, knowing their parents would always be there for them. My best guess was that the only way they'd survived with any kind of sanity intact was because they'd had each other.

They didn't need me to be a part of their reunion, especially since I wasn't their family — and never would be. I needed to go. If Sebastian took me home now, I'd have enough time to do a few chores and make myself some dinner before diving into work. I didn't have royalties to live on and publicists didn't usually make seven-figure incomes. I had to get my head back in the game.

From my seat on the sofa, I watched a few more seconds as they interacted. Then I leaned forward to get their attention. "I should probably get going. I wasn't planning on taking an entire day off."

Sebastian checked the time on his cell. "I was going to get started on dinner in a few minutes. I can take you home after."

I wrinkled my nose. "Or you could take me home now. I still have work I really need to get done today."

He swiveled back to India. "I'll be back in a half hour or so. You'll be fine while I'm gone?"

India gave him a boys-are-so-stupid smile and patted his cheek. "I've been on my own for three years."

He didn't turn back around and I couldn't see his face, but the air thickened and India's face sobered. "You promise you'll be here when I get back?"

She grinned. "I don't have a car and I doubt I'll get very far dragging around two big suitcases. I'll be here. I promise."

He rose, closed the distance between us and held out his hand to me. I took it and he levered me up. We stood toe-to-toe, our faces inches apart. I broke eye contact first and plucked my purse from beside the couch.

"It was really great meeting you, India. I'm sure I'll see you soon."

She bounced off the couch and dashed over to me, folding me into a hug and squeezing hard. "Thank you so much. For everything."

"You're very welcome." I held her face and

turned it down to drop a kiss on her forehead. "You two be good to each other."

Fifteen minutes later, Sebastian pulled the Land Rover into my driveway. "Thanks for the ride." I hopped out, hoping for my sake that would be the end of it and he'd take off. Instead, he killed the engine and got out. Damn. I needed to make things clear to him, let him know that whatever had started couldn't continue. I barreled toward my little house, thinking he'd get the hint and leave. But he didn't.

"Violet."

I halted just before I got to the door and spun around to face him, trying to keep a casual air. He'd just reunited with his sister. He didn't need me causing that perfect little bubble to explode. "Thanks for the ride," I echoed.

One side of his mouth curved up and he entwined his fingers through mine, then he brought our joined hands to his chest. "Thanks so much for what you did today."

"I loved every minute of it. Seeing you two together —" My breath caught in my throat as his neck arched downward and his lips brushed the top of my hand.

He released my hand, but snagged an arm around my waist, throwing me against his chest. "I downright detest you right now."

"And I'm pretty sure I hate you," I said on a breathy sigh.

As his body shifted against mine, his fingers weaved through my hair and curled around my neck. Pressing his forehead to mine, he shut his eyes. "Tell me who the father is. I need to know who I'm competing against."

Tears sprang from my eyes. He deserved to know the truth, but what if something unforeseen happened in the next few weeks? Then he'd mourn the loss of his baby. He didn't need that kind of grief. I'd wait until after the first trimester, before allowing him to become emotionally invested. I had to power through the next three weeks and then he'd know everything.

I laughed to lighten the mood. "Don't worry, I can't think of any other man I dislike as much as you."

His mouth crashed down on mine and we fell against the door. I swallowed his sexy moan with a deeper kiss, rolling my tongue against his and running my hands up his muscular back.

Oh, hell. I wasn't supposed to be kissing him. I disentangled myself from him, shaking my head. "Okay, well..."

He chuckled. "I'll call you later tonight and let you know how everything went with India."

I grinned, unable to dodge his infectious attitude.

"Good. Do that." I waved and disappeared into my house. Once inside, I let my purse drop to the floor as I leaned against the door.

I'd been trying to resist Sebastian, telling myself we weren't right for each other. Instead, I'd let myself fall completely in love with him.

I was in so much trouble.

CHAPTER FOURTEEN

★ *Sebastian* ★

When I steered the Land Rover into my driveway, I immediately saw Theo's old Corvette. Damn, I did not want that guy alone with my sister. Though Theo had seemed to mellow out over the last couple of months — he'd gotten the same verbal lashing from Liam that had inspired my rehab trip — I still didn't trust him with women, especially not my little sister.

I shoved the door open to find them in the living room with plenty of space between them. They definitely hadn't been doing what I'd been doing with Violet. I rolled my shoulders in a circle, crossed the room and fist-bumped with Theo. "Hey, man, what's up?"

India popped off the couch. "You two do whatever. I'm going to start unpacking. Nice to see you again, Theo."

"Wow, I didn't expect to see India. When did this happen?"

I sat across from him on the coffee table. "Just this morning." I left it at that because Theo wasn't a chick. If he wanted to know more, he'd ask. "What brings you by?"

"Checkin' in on you. Violet's kept you so busy, we've barely heard a peep from you." A mischievous smile took over his face. "Guess you guys are getting along pretty good, huh?"

I'd never been big on kissing and telling, but how the hell did Theo know anything at all? Even if Liam, Faith or Emma mentioned Violet being here last night, we definitely hadn't acted at all like a couple. "We're working together. What makes you think anything else is going on?"

He threw his head back and laughed. "You're kidding, right?"

Baffled, I blinked. "No, I'm not. What am I missing?"

The smile slowly faded and he tilted his head. "Are you seriously denying that you slept with her?"

I scratched my chin, my brows inching lower. "Yes."

His mouth dropped open and he shook his head, raising his palms to face me. "Hold on. So you're saying that when I came to check on you the next morning after Liam cut you from the band, Violet wasn't doing the walk of shame down your driveway and slinking into her car?"

"Violet's never been here that early in the morning, and she sure as hell didn't do a walk of shame." Maybe Theo had been seeing things. "You sure you were at the right house?"

"Sebastian"—he leaned forward and gripped my arm—"I knew how to get to your other house. Aidan hadn't heard from Violet and her car hadn't been parked at the house when he arrived from the airport around six-thirty that morning. He had an important meeting across town with a client at eight, so he asked me to drop by your place since I lived so close to you. I got right out of bed and raced over—just after seven, too early for Violet to be coming over on business. I saw her sneaking *out* of your house, that red hair all over the place and looking like she was making a getaway. No one else, no mistake."

Violet had spent the night at my house? Why didn't I know this? Well, obviously I'd just forgotten, because I'd been so wasted.

An image of Violet assaulted my brain, her naked with me on the bed, my hands full of her breasts. And she felt *amazing*. I'd had a few flashes of images before and thought they were just my torrid thoughts running away from me. Were those pictures real memories and not my imagination? Her face swam before me again, her eyes smoldering as she climbed over me and straddled my hips. Naked.

Yep, we'd had sex.

I darted to the calendar hanging on the side of the fridge. She'd said she was nine weeks pregnant. I flipped the pages back. Nine weeks took me back to right around the time Liam had ousted me from the band. Either Violet had been with another guy within days of being with me — she didn't seem like the type for one reckless encounter, much less two — or the father of the baby was me.

Gulp.

My stomach bottomed out and I sucked in air like I'd just been under water for an eternity. I had talked about having a family one day, looked forward to it. But right now? And did I want that with Violet? A few hours ago, I was certain I wanted to be with her and be a stepfather to her baby. *Surprise!* I wouldn't have been just the stepfather, but the actual father.

"You okay, bro?" Theo slapped me on the back and I realized I'd bent over, my hands levered against my knees while I struggled to catch my breath.

I was going to be a dad. With Violet.

Violet, who had known for days that I was the father and couldn't be bothered to tell me. Violet, who'd let me believe that some other guy had slept with her, some other guy had made a baby with her. Violet, who I had opened up to and who had dodged my questions. When was she going to tell me I was *that* guy? Was she going to wait until she was about to give birth? Or had she planned to keep me in the dark even then?

"Dude, do I need to call an ambulance or something?" Theo patted my back again. "You're worrying me."

I straightened, composed myself and looked Theo in the eye. "Nah, I'm fine. I think it was a flashback from all that garbage we ingested in Cabo last year."

"What's this 'we' crap? I wasn't stupid enough to touch any of that poison." He bobbed his head closer, narrowing his eyes. "You sure you're okay?"

"I'm good." I forced my face into some kind of normalcy, though I felt anything but composed. I wanted to peel out of my driveway and storm into her house and demand to know why she'd kept the baby from me. But I wouldn't. I'd stew on it a while, plan a rational attack. "So, how is everyone? Brett measuring up all right?"

"Yeah, he's good. A little soft, but the chicks like him. And when I say 'soft' I mean he's way too good. For a while there, I even suspected he was still a virgin."

"I doubt that." I laughed. "Want a beer?"

"You still keep beer in the fridge? You don't find it tempting?"

"Not at all." I fetched him a bottle, flipped off the

top and handed it to him. "Not into it. I've been on both sides of the fence and I've chosen the side I like best."

"Good to hear." He meandered into the living room and I followed him. He glanced toward the arched doorway where my sister had vanished.

"By the way, she's off limits to you. Just saying." I jerked my head toward my sister's room. "Don't even think about going there."

"Zero interest, bro. I grew up with her, just like you did. She's like a baby sister to me." He shook his head. "Besides, if I was into dating my friends' sisters, I'd hook up with Faith."

"Liam's Faith?" My eyes bugged out and my body shook with laughter. "Oh, I hope you do try something, because the fireworks from that show would be absolutely mesmerizing. Wait." I punched him in the shoulder. "You grew up with Faith, too."

"Not the same at all. She was two years older and almost never around. Always had a boyfriend or she was out with her hot friends. I didn't really grow up with her. On the contrary, I grew up worshipping her."

"You are so screwed." I sent my knuckles into his arm.

"Who's screwed?" India strolled into the living room.

I glanced at Theo and he shook his head. "No one," I answered her. "Theo, are you staying for dinner?"

"Don't be a moron."

That meant yes. Good, between Theo, India and my cooking task at hand, I might be distracted enough to keep myself from beating down Violet's door.

★

My sleep sucked and I woke the next morning more tired than when I'd gone to bed. All the thoughts that had followed me to bed had festered and ripened into a big, explosive bomb, ready to detonate. By the time I crawled out of bed, I'd built Violet into a total villain. I mean, why not? I should've followed my original instinct that she was cold and bitchy. Whatever. I wasn't going to waste any more time on someone who didn't think I was worth being a part of my own child's life.

Except that I had to hash it out with her at some point. She was carrying my child and no way would I let her cut me out. I wanted to be a part of my kid's life. But not yet. Violet was only a couple of months along. I still had six or seven months before I even met the child.

I didn't trust myself to talk to her in person. The urge to beat down her door and storm into her house, maybe even scream some choice curse words, raged through my veins. Since my anger was building, I didn't know how not to explode. She and the baby didn't need the added stress.

But I had to say something or I was going to burst. As I grabbed my toothbrush, I knew I couldn't hold back. The fuse had already been lit and the bomb in my head was about to go off. I tossed the toothbrush into the sink and went in search of my phone.

Why didn't you tell me I was the father? I texted her. No point in beating around the bush. *You know what? Never mind. Any excuse you give me won't mean anything anyway.* I sent the text, then stared at the screen, so very far from being satisfied. After a beat, I typed out, *You're fired*, then turned off my phone and chucked it on my bed. Screw her.

"Good morning." India poked her head into my doorway, a grin waiting for me. "I was thinking about making pancakes. Hungry?"

"Yes." I eyed my phone, wondering if Violet would come looking for me once she realized I'd turned off my phone. For all I knew, she was already on her way. "Let's go out to eat. Be ready in five." I shut the door in her face and busted my ass to get ready, racing against time. I didn't want to be here when Violet showed up. In fact, a trip out of town sounded like a good idea. "Pack some overnight stuff. I want to take you somewhere."

CHAPTER FIFTEEN
★ Violet ★

One full week. That's how long Sebastian's phone had been turned off. The same amount of time his Land Rover had been missing — as near as I could tell every time I'd let myself through his gate and peeked into the window of his garage. Which, embarrassingly, was about twice a day.

And today was no different. I scanned the grounds, looking for any sign he'd been home. A flyer had been wedged on the latch of the gate the other day and it was still sitting in the exact same spot. Sebastian didn't like clutter. He would've picked it off if he'd seen it, which told me he hadn't been anywhere near his house.

I eased my exhausted body back behind the wheel and dropped my head against the back of the seat. What was I supposed to do? I'd already rescheduled three appearances and a telephone interview. But should I also reschedule the ones I'd arranged over the last few days?

After rummaging through my purse again for my phone, I turned on speech-to-text. "This is ridiculous. I'd planned on waiting until after twelve weeks before telling anyone. Even you."

If only India had a phone. But she didn't, so I had no way to reach either of them. They were obviously together, because she hadn't been home either and I couldn't see Sebastian leaving town without her so soon after getting her back. "If I don't hear from you by tonight, I'm going to start calling hospitals." I clicked Send and tossed my phone on the passenger seat, started up the Lexus and cruised out of his driveway.

Stupid Sebastian. But that hadn't stopped me from falling for him. I pounded a fist into the steering wheel and wiped the tears dribbling down my cheek. I missed him. I missed ogling his stomach — and the rest of him. I missed his sense of humor, the way he took care of me and, damn it, I missed his cooking. Mostly, I missed the way he looked at me, the way his eyes smoldered when he wanted to kiss me.

Thirty minutes later, I was making myself a salad when three knocks sounded at the door. I dropped the metal mixing bowl with a clatter and rocketed to the door. I opened it, ready to hug Sebastian. My face fell.

"Dad, what's up?" My shoulders sagged as I shuffled back to the kitchen, knowing he'd follow.

"Just checking on you."

I scooped a generous portion of salad onto my plate. "Want some?"

"Rabbit food?" He snickered. "No, thanks."

I grabbed a fork and slid onto a stool. "So what brings you by? For real."

He leaned on the counter at my side. "Worried about you. Sure you have everything under control?"

"Yes, Dad." I sighed at his lack of faith. "It's just a little hiccup. I'll make it happen, just like I always do."

"Good. Then you won't freak when I tell you that Sebastian called and asked me to relay a message to you. He says he'll be home in a few days and to please reschedule all his appearances for next week, anytime after Monday." He beat his fingernails on the counter. "And, uh..."

"That message doesn't seem freak-worthy. Is there more?" I prayed Sebastian hadn't told my dad about the baby. I didn't want him finding out from someone else.

"He requests that you stop calling him."

My face flushed as embarrassment smothered me like an icky rag. Great, now I looked like a pathetic girl chasing after some idiot guy. Worse, I was still working for Sebastian after he'd fired me. But I was confident that once he heard me out, he would unfire me. "I'm not stalking him, Dad. We're working together. I can't do my job without him." I clenched my jaw. "What a jerk."

"Look, honey, I'm not an idiot."

I prayed he hadn't figured out I was pregnant. I'd just die. I mean, he needed to know at some point and pretty soon, because I couldn't hide it for long. But I hoped by then, I had a plan together for my future, so I didn't look like a total loser. "I know you're not an idiot, Dad."

"Then why do you keep acting like I'm supposed to believe you when you say everything's fine?"

I chewed my lip, knowing I had to tell him. But I wanted to put it off as long as possible. "I'm sorry. I don't think you're stupid. I'm just not ready to talk about it yet."

"When your mother took you away and I had no way to find you..." He swallowed and closed his eyes a moment before they landed square on me. "I'm afraid I'm losing you again. I know I'm not big on the hugs and mushy words. But, honey, I'd die if anything happened to you."

Tears sprang from my eyes and I threw myself at him, wrapping my arms around his neck. "I'm not sick or anything." I sniffed and released him. "Just pregnant. I was too embarrassed to tell you."

And I bawled. My shoulders shook and I knew my face was getting hideously splotchy. The ugly cry. Yay.

Dad stroked my back until the sobbing subsided. "I'm going to be a grandpa."

I could hear the smile in his voice. I grabbed a tissue and laughed. "Yes, you are."

"Do I know the father?"

"Yes, you do." I cleared my throat. My dad deserved to know why he'd been thrown in the middle of the war between Sebastian and me, didn't he?

Taking a deep breath, I started at the beginning.

CHAPTER SIXTEEN
★ *Sebastian* ★

I *surveyed the* inside of The Wagon Wheel. Families ate at tables, singles crowded the bar and leather-clad guys and tattooed women played pool at the far end of the spacious saloon. I could see why Liam had stayed here so long. The place was hopping for a Tuesday evening, and in a small town like Gardnerville, Nevada no less. Even better, they were about to get karaoke going. I hoped to get India up on that stage. I glanced at the stool next to me where she played on my phone. I'd have to get her one of her own. Soon.

"Hi, I'm Marianne. Anytime you need something, I'm your girl. Can I start you off with a drink?"

"I'm good with iced tea."

"Hi." India smiled up at Marianne. "I'll have the same. And a burger with everything."

I grinned. "I'll have the same."

The waitress turned to go, then doubled back

and eyed me. "You're one of the guys from Full Throttle?"

I nodded, but I wasn't too worried about being rushed. Out in Hollywood, the paparazzi had fallen in love with me when I'd made it to the Most Beautiful people list. But as a front man, Liam was much better known, which left me more likely to safely navigate the crowds of small towns easily without being mauled.

"Be right back with your drinks." She swung around and disappeared into the crowd.

A few minutes after the waitress dropped off our drinks, one of the other chairs at our table scraped across the floor, and a gorgeous brunette claimed the chair. "I thought I made it clear we didn't want Liam or his kind around here?"

I chuckled. "Then stop tempting us with all this." I waved my hand to encompass the entire saloon.

"I'm Breanna." She held out her hand to me, then India. "Staying at Emma's old place?"

"Yes, but I got roped into doing some house repairs while I'm there." I scoffed playfully. "I probably would've been better off at a hotel."

"Probably." She grinned. "I'm visiting Emma in a few weeks. You guys have any gigs in the area soon?"

"No, but Aidan could arrange something if the rest of the guys are up for it." I glanced over at the stage. "You're managing this place right now, yeah?"

"Until the owner comes back from sabbatical." She scowled. "I think I liked waitressing better. More action."

"Maybe you need more to do. Like get us a song list?" I snuck a peek at India who was on my phone, engrossed with reading memes. "And you could let us slide if we do something that isn't country."

"I gotcha covered." She flashed me a smile, stood and pushed the chair back in. "Be right back."

Because I was a guy and I loved gawking at a hot girl as much as the next guy, I checked her out as she sashayed to the stage, weaving between tables. My gaze drifted away and I slumped a little lower in my chair. No matter how great Breanna looked in that short skirt, I'd still rather look at Violet.

India placed my phone on the bar. "You're not thinking about her again, are you?"

I laughed once, trying to cover my discomfort. "Who?"

"Are you ever going to tell me what spooked you?" India rolled her eyes when I shook my head. "Sebastian, why the hell are we still in the middle of nowhere? Don't get me wrong, I love this town. And I'm grateful to spend time with you. But you're supposed to be cleaning up your image, remember? You can't do that from here. You need to be home, seeing and being seen."

Breanna slipped the karaoke list in front of me and then disappeared again.

"Thanks," I called out.

"You're going to sing?" India asked with a frown.

"I'm not singing. You are." I slid the paper across the table until it sat right in front of her.

She drew in a long, shaky breath and stared at the piece of paper as if it were a dirty toilet. "I haven't sang in a while."

"Well," I softened my voice, "you sounded pretty amazing last time I heard you."

"What if I'm not anymore, though?" Her eyes found me. "What if I suck?"

"Doll, if you're even half as good as you used to be, you're going to bring the house down."

She beamed. "You thought I was that good?"

"No way." I shook my head. "I thought you were that *great*."

She covered my hand with both of hers. "You're a good brother, you know? You always were."

I layered my free hand over hers. "You make it easy. Thank you for coming back to me."

"You're welcome." She grinned. "Now tell me what happened with Violet."

I groaned. "We're back to that?"

"And we'll keep coming back to it until you deliver the goods." Her eyes widened as Marianne slid a plate in front of her. "Ooh, will ya look at that."

"Thank you," I told the waitress as she delivered my burger. "Okay."

"You're going to tell me?" She set down her burger and her eyes snapped to mine.

I lifted the top bun and squeezed ketchup onto the patty. "She withheld information, something I deserved to know. I didn't appreciate it."

"And you fired her." India bit into the burger and sauce dripped out the bottom. "Without even talking to her about it."

"What's to talk about?" Damn, and now I wasn't really all that hungry for the burger. "She did what she did. Not cool. I walked. End of story."

"But you love her." India poked me in the chest. "You're in love with her, yet you didn't think she deserved the chance to defend herself. Worse, you did it over text. Lame, bro. Really lame."

"But you don't know what she did. How can I be the one at fault when *you* only know half the story?" I pushed my plate away.

"Same way you can lay the blame on her when you only know half the story." She smirked. "I'm not saying you're wrong. I'm just saying you didn't give her a chance. Maybe what she did was wrong, maybe not. I don't know. But you have to take the time to hear her side, understand why she did it. Hey, she's probably not perfect and I haven't known her long at all. But I'll never forget how safe she made me feel. I've been around bad people, Sebastian, we both have. I know the difference. They aren't capable of that kind of caring."

My throat burned in frustration. Damn, Violet had really whipped me. Worse, I wanted so badly to hear her out, let her convince me she didn't do anything wrong. I wanted her to be the girl of my dreams. Hell, before I'd figured out her deception, she *was* the girl of my dreams. Maybe she still was...

"Okay. We'll leave in the morning." I'd see Violet right away. And even if she didn't tell me what I wanted to hear and I lost hope, at least maybe I'd be able to move on. Appetite restored, I took a giant-sized bite of the burger.

"No offense, Sebastian, but you've been really rotten company since we left L.A. I vote we leave after dinner, go directly to Violet's and see how this plays out."

I shook my head. "I'm not arriving on her doorstep at eleven and getting her out of a deep sleep."

One side of India's mouth curled up, one brow raised. "Have you looked at the timestamps on the texts she sends you every night? She's not sleeping well. Maybe a good conversation might help with her insomnia."

Violet had been up at all hours? Sleep deprivation wasn't good for the baby. *Our* baby. Aw, hell, I needed to get back to Los Angeles.

CHAPTER SEVENTEEN

★ *Violet* ★

And still no Sebastian. Where the hell had he gone? And it was ten o'clock at night, for crying out loud. Why was I at his place again instead of sleeping?

Because being home and trying to fall asleep at a normal hour was pointless.

I started up my car and was about to turn left and go back home. Steering the opposite direction, I headed to Faith's. We'd talked a lot over the last couple years. Well, not a lot, but some. Certainly more than I'd talked with other women. I'd been too focused on my education and career to make a lot of friends. But I'd always liked Faith. She was adventurous and she'd grown up with Liam, Theo and Sebastian. Maybe she'd know where he went. Besides, when I'd seen her at Sebastian's house the other day, she had suggested we hang out.

I parked on the street in front of her house,

praying she was still up. The light was on in the dining room and shadows passed over the curtain. I was in luck. Before I got a chance to knock, Faith flung the door open. "Hey, Violet. What's going on?"

Not knowing where to even begin, I looked to the dark sky and blew a raspberry.

She gave me a sympathetic smile. "Come inside and tell me all about it. Don't mind the mess. I have a three-year-old. He's sleeping right now though. Good move on your part avoiding the chaos."

Toys littered the floor of her small house and the kitchen looked like a chemist was having a party. I made my way to the counter. "Making meth?"

She threw her head back and laughed. "Homemade vanilla extract. As soon as I get that going, I'm moving onto organic facial wash."

"Wow." I stooped down to sniff a small bottle. "Patchouli?"

"The nose knows." She giggled at her lame joke and washed her hands in the kitchen sink. "It's very therapeutic. It can be used as a fungicidal or deodorant and it heals a myriad of skin problems."

I inhaled over another bottle. Lavender, my favorite.

She dried her hands on a towel. "I'm thinking this isn't a social call and I seriously doubt you came all the way over here to sniff my stuff. What gives?"

"Sebastian isn't speaking to me." I groaned and hung my head, reluctant to tell anyone too much. "He just disappeared with India and no one's heard from him. Except my dad who he told to relay a message to me. Wasn't friendly either."

She slid onto a stool at the kitchen counter. "And he's not talking to you because...?"

Tugging my ears, I studied the plain white ceiling as I decided on the proper wording. "I kept certain pieces of information from him and he's pissed about it."

Faith pursed her lips. "I'm getting the feeling that it's information you want to keep from me as well. Rather than me try to pry it out of you, why don't you just skip to the good parts and hit me with the real problem?"

"No problem, really. Not that can be solved. I just needed a sounding board." At her hand flourish, I continued. "See, I like Sebastian. Too much actually. But we're not right for each other and —"

"Wait," she interrupted. "Why aren't you right for each other?"

I shrugged. "For starters, he's a celebrity and I don't date actors or musicians."

She snorted. "As well you shouldn't. That's just sound judgment. Go on."

"And we're not at all alike. He's laid-back and I'm extremely organized with attention to detail."

"You can say it, Violet." Faith smirked. "Anal. Say it with me."

"Fine. I'm anal." I emptied my lungs with a whoosh. "And I'm afraid he won't be able to keep up. You know, I've got a masters degree and he barely made it through high school."

She nodded, pursing her lips. "So you don't think he's smart enough for you."

"I don't know. I just don't want to be in a relationship where I'm doing all the thinking." There, I'd said it. And, yes, I felt like an ass. I knew Sebastian wasn't a moron, but I just couldn't let go of my lifelong fantasy of having an astoundingly intelligent guy who could keep up with my logic.

"Well, let me ask you. Can you play guitar?"

I hesitated, wondering why she was asking me such a ridiculous question. "No."

"Can you write lyrics?" she asked. I shook my head. "Or write music to go along with the words, arrange the chords and all that?"

I moaned. "Where is this going?"

"Would you have been able to survive if you'd been on your own at eighteen?" she asked. I didn't bother answering that question and she didn't wait for one. "Could you fix your car if it broke down or handle a leaky pipe on your own?"

I didn't answer any of the questions. Since all answers were an obvious no, I assumed her questions were rhetorical. Silence from Faith, finally. Realizing I probably wouldn't leave for a few more minutes, I slid onto the stool next to her, waiting for her to fire the next question.

"How many highly educated people — lawyers, doctors, engineers — have you met who are happier than the rest of us? Doesn't mean a thing, only that they have potential to make more money. And we all know that doesn't buy happiness." She paused, tilting her head as if measuring her next words. "I've known Sebastian a long time. He's made plenty of mistakes, but he's also learned what not to do. And despite his awful childhood, he figured out how to rise above it and be happy. How many people in this world are smart enough to figure out how to live an honest life where they can be genuinely happy? Everyone has their own brand of smart. You're book smart. He's life smart."

She waited, letting that sink in and then continued. "He'd never try to be as organized as you or try to make decisions on public relations. And you could never compete with him on other levels. Sebastian is gifted, make no mistake about that."

I whined, an ache beginning in my heart and seeping into my stomach. My legs were feeling it too, the new awareness sucking away all my energy. I wasn't sure if I could drag my ass to my car. I stared down at the counter, seeing nothing but Sebastian smiling at me, being sweet to me, composing a beautiful song. "I've been such a loser."

"Nah. A total loser wouldn't have come over here for my wise words of wisdom." She grinned. "And on the other matter, why don't you date celebrities or musicians?"

I rolled my eyes. "Oh, please. They're self-absorbed, think they're better than everyone else and... well, isn't that enough?"

Faith slowly moved her head up and down. "You don't look in the mirror much, do you?"

Did she really just imply that I thought I was better than other people?

But wasn't that what I'd been doing with Sebastian? And I was *not* better than him. He was generous and kind, all the best traits I was apparently devoid of. I groaned and banged my forehead on the counter. "Guess I'm not as smart as I thought. Because if I had any brains at all, I would've taken all that into account and I wouldn't have thrown him away like that. I'm a complete dumbass."

"That you are."

I lifted my head and gave her the death glare. "You're not helping."

"Of course I am." She shot me a smug smile. "You arrived here all lost. And now you know what you need to do. Grovel at his feet. A lot."

Yes, I knew what I needed to do. Renewed

purpose shot adrenaline through me. "You're the best." I hopped off the stool and threw my arms around her. "I'll let you know how it goes."

"You'd better."

I swung the door open, then called over my shoulder, "And I want some of that facial wash."

"Wait!" She rounded the counter, plucking up a tiny brown bottle, and thrust it at me. "Vanilla bean extract. He likes to cook. Maybe this will butter him up."

Ten minutes later, I veered to the side and stopped at the curb. I rummaged through my purse for my cell and found Sebastian's text thread. *Please call me. Please. At least give me a chance to explain.* I sent the text, then waited a moment. There had to be something else I could say, something that would show why he should listen to me. *I hate you. I mean I really, really detest you.*

He'd know what I really meant, that I was falling in love with him. I'd opened myself to all kinds of hurt, given him a way to break me. I prayed he wouldn't, that he was too generous to rub it in. I hoped he cared about me even half as much as I cared for him.

As soon as I walked into my house, I jumped into the shower. I left my hair dripping while I put on some water to boil for lemon tea.

It had been an hour and Sebastian hadn't

answered my text. If he still cared about me, if he was open to hearing from me, if there was any hope for us, wouldn't he have answered that text?

Sitting at the dining room table, I brought my legs up, folded my arms around them, and then I rested my forehead on my knees. He was probably out partying with some hot girl, maybe even drinking. Maybe even *touching* her. Probably touching her a lot.

Pounding at the door had me jumping and when the heel of my foot slid off the edge of the chair, I almost fell off. What the hell was my dad doing up this late? I stumbled to the door and flung it open.

I stared at the tall, dark figure at my door. "Sebastian," I whispered. "I'm so sorry." And the waterworks started. Damn hormones. "Please let me explain what happened."

His face remained immobile, emotionless. "I'm here, aren't I?"

Behind Sebastian at the end of the driveway, the LR4 peeled out. "Wasn't that your car?" I asked.

"Yes. With my cell phone in it." Sebastian stared at the empty street and scratched his head. "I can't even call India to tell her to get her ass back here."

I suppressed a smile and headed to the kitchen, waiting for him to follow me. "I was just making some tea. Want some?"

"No." His voice took on a hard edge. "I need you

to say what you have to say so I can go."

My fingers froze around the teapot handle. He wasn't going to make this easy for me. Fine. I'd be honest and speak from my heart. And if he still didn't want me, then I'd eventually convince myself that it wasn't meant to be. But I wasn't going to hurry so he could leave any sooner. I lifted the teapot and carefully, very carefully so my trembling hands wouldn't miss and spill boiling water all over the counter, poured the water into my mug.

I took a deep, cleansing breath and went for it. "See, when I started working with you, I was pissed. Because you acted like what had happened meant nothing to you." I swished the teabag around, peeking up at him from under my lashes. I couldn't tell what he was thinking. He was unreadable. "And, secretly, I kind of liked you. That you didn't acknowledge our night together, and didn't seem to care at all, well, it made me feel small and insignificant. I was hurt. And to cover that up, I behaved badly."

"None of that explains why you purposely withheld the fact that you're carrying *my* child."

I held up one finger. "I'm getting there." Needing another moment to gather my wits, I squeezed lemon into the mug, then took my time getting the first sip.

"Can you speed things up? I have a long walk home." He folded his arms over his chest.

I leaned a hip against the counter. "When you first suspected I was pregnant and asked if I'd been with anyone, that was the moment I realized you didn't remember that night at all. Talk about feeling unmemorable." I gave a watery laugh.

"So it was revenge?" Sebastian's eyes darkened.

"No, Sebastian, not revenge." I sat the mug down with a bang. "I didn't even know I was pregnant."

He blinked. "You could have told me later. Or were you not sure I was the father?"

"Excuse me?" I straightened. "I haven't been with anyone except you in forever." This wasn't going well and my throat burned, my eyes stung. I took another sip from my mug, closed my eyes and tried to make peace with the fact that Sebastian probably didn't want me anymore. And wasn't knowing that better than not knowing? I needed him to be really honest about how he felt. "You were so sweet and my little crush started getting out of hand. And... I was afraid."

"Afraid?" He unfolded his arms and rested a fist on the counter.

"I realized you were a really decent guy. I loved being around you and the more time I spent with you, the harder I fell." Oh, God, did I really just admit to that? "Like I said, you're a decent guy. And the good guys try to do the right thing." My lips trembled, but I braved the humiliation, the truth.

"What if I told you about the baby and you wanted to do the right thing? What if you were with me only out of obligation?"

Blasted tears spurted out of my eyes and I quickly turned away from Sebastian to wipe them. "I couldn't bear caring about you and never truly knowing how you felt, always wondering if my feelings were returned. I planned to tell you as soon as I had everything sorted out between us, as soon as I knew if your feelings were genuine or if you were just being kind to the miserable pregnant lady."

There, I'd said it all. I kept my back to him, because I didn't want to see the expression on his face. I couldn't even imagine what was going through his head. I mean, he was a brilliant rock star and could have any girl he wanted.

The heat from his body warmed me as he slowly slipped an arm around my waist to splay his hand over my stomach. "I'm sorry. Sorry for getting so drunk and being such a mess that I didn't remember. I'm sorry you had to go through these last few weeks alone and I'm sorry for bailing without giving you a chance to give me your side."

I moved backward into him and rested my hands on his wrists, uncertain whether leaning into his embrace would push him away or make him bolt. "Do not, *do not* feel sorry for me. I did this. I knew you were beyond wasted and I stayed. I have no one to blame but myself." I filled my lungs with air as if it would give me strength. "I'm not an obligation or a duty to uphold."

"Never." Sebastian chuckled as he gently brushed my hair off my shoulder. "You're smart, sexy and since the moment you walked into my house with that dreadful list, I haven't been able to get you out of my head. And now, at the risk of sounding super cheesy, I can't get you out of my heart."

I pressed my lips together to keep from laughing. "Wow, that *was* super cheesy."

"Baby, you have me so whipped, cheesy is all I'm capable of." He gently nudged me away, and spun me around to face him.

"You're like whipped cheese." I chuckled at my bad joke and instead of laughing, he scooped me up into his arms and carried me out of the kitchen. "What are you doing?"

He hauled me to the living room and carefully deposited me onto the couch. Cupping both sides of my face, he planted the softest of kisses on my forehead, my chin, both my cheeks and then my lips. When I opened my eyes, he was staring at me.

"I'm going to take care of you. Not because I have to, but because I want to." Sebastian brushed my lips again, then kneeled on the floor in front of me. "Because I hurt you and somehow, you eventually found the strength to let it go. Because you took care of my sister, made sure I didn't lose her again. You made her feel safe and if not for you, I may not have had the chance to prove to her she could trust me. Because you're the most amazing woman I've ever known. And I don't want to be without you."

My heart swelled with love and I pressed his hand between mine. "Wow, I'm really hating on you right now. You disgust me."

He grinned. "Ditto."

"I hate you so much, I refuse to give you a ride home."

He shrugged. "Guess I'm stuck here."

"That's just awful." The amusement waned and I rose, tugging on his hand until he stood too. I slid my hands over his chest, around his shoulders and planted them behind his head. "I've learned a lot these past few weeks. The most important thing: I seriously don't want to be without you either." But that wasn't enough. I needed him to know how much I valued him, that I admired and respected him, that I didn't think I was better than him. "I have a confession."

Sebastian's hand froze at my waist. "What is it?"

"I'm ridiculously in love with you. Have been for a while." I braced myself, knowing that it was probably way too soon for him to say it back. He'd gotten close enough. "Are you sure you want to do this with me, be a family?"

"Positive. I've never wanted anything more. You, the baby — I want the whole package."

I smiled, wanting more but knowing that had to be enough for me.

"I love our baby. Hell, I loved the baby when I thought someone else was the father. But I loved *you* before that." He cupped my face, his thumb brushing my bottom lip.

Yeah, that was good. I beamed. "Okay."

"Okay." He kissed me, his mouth testing mine, exploring. I opened for him, letting the taste of him seep into me. In that moment, I knew there was no part of him — his body or his heart — that he hadn't given to me willingly.

I had thought that I knew what I needed and had meticulously planned my life years in advance. Instead, I found the love of my life and would soon have his child. In the end, I got what really mattered.

The End

If you enjoyed this book, please recommend it to friends, reader's groups and discussion boards or tell others how much you enjoyed it by reviewing it on Amazon, GoodReads or your own site. Thank you and happy reading!

★

Books in the Rock Star Kisses series:

The Runaway Rock Star

BOOK ONE

The Baby and the Rock Star
BOOK TWO

Tempting the Rock Star
BOOK THREE

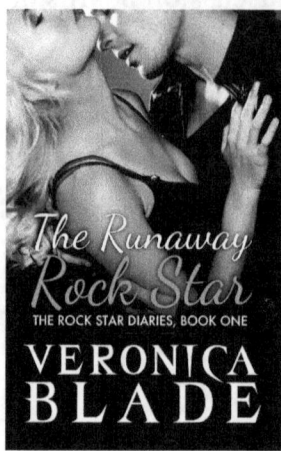
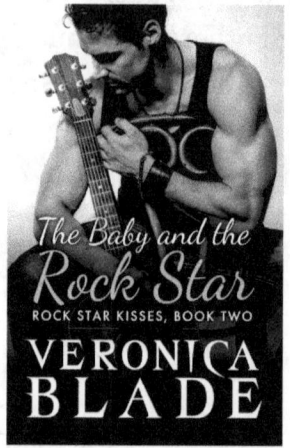

More Titles by Veronica Blade

Should a woman who's unable to forget her first love give "happily ever after" one more try?

When good-girl Maddie switches places with her famous bad-girl twin Jackie, she has some pretty high stilettos to fill.

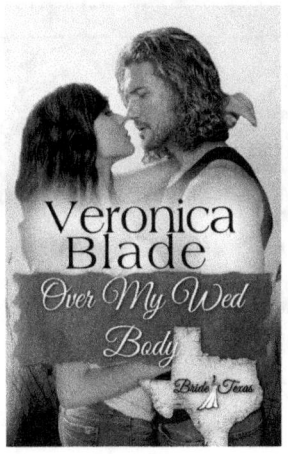

When Hunter realizes he botched the annulment of his marriage to his longtime friend, he must decide if she and their marriage are worth fighting for.

A micro trilogy including Single-Handed, Singled Out (book two) & Single-minded (book three).

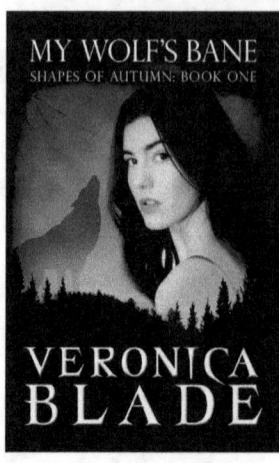

Thrown to the Wolves:
The Legend of Hannah & Eli (prequel)

My Wolf's Bane (book one)

Wolves at the Door
(book two)

Dead Wolf Walking
(book three)

The Dark Wolf (book four)

Lord of the Wolves (book five)

Different species. Mortal enemies. It'll never work, but they'll die trying.

Free e-Book Offer

For a limited time, *Thrown To The Wolves: The Legend of Hannah & Eli (Shapes of Autumn Prequel)* is available for free from my website.

Find out more at VeronicaBlade.com

More Titles by Veronica Blade

A newbie witch enlists help from the scrumptious school bad-boy to make her life and death choice between two battling covens.

The witch queen must make the impossible choice between abandoning the throne and her people, or spending eternity with the man she loves.

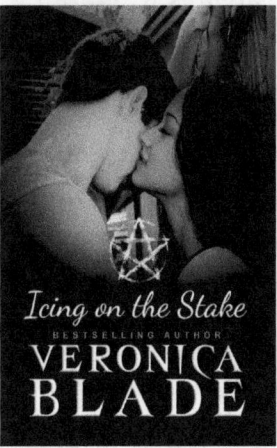

Sofia lays her hard-won anonymity on the line by saving the most popular boy in school. Worse, she's been exposed to the vampire hunters who attacked him.

A Cinderella who spends her nights as a wolf. A prince with a taste for blood.

About Veronica Blade

Veronica Blade lives near Carson City, Nevada with her husband and furbabies but also spends a lot of time in southern California. She writes sweet romances to live vicariously through her characters. Except her heroes and heroines lead far more interesting lives—and they are always way hotter.

★

You can visit Veronica Blade on Facebook, check out her website or follow her on Twitter. You can even e-mail her at veronica@veronicablade.com. She loves hearing from readers!

www.ingramcontent.com/pod-product-compliance
Lightning Source LLC
Chambersburg PA
CBHW061143170626
46809CB00003B/966